Gift of the Ancients

Future Past

BIANCA D'ARC

This book is a work of fiction. The names, characters, places, and incidents are products of the writer's imagination or have been used fictitiously and are not to be construed as real. Any resemblance to persons, living or dead, actual events, locale or organizations is entirely coincidental.

No part of this book may be used or reproduced in any manner whatsoever without written permission, except in the case of brief quotations embodied in critical articles and reviews.

They can see the future, but can they outrun the past?

Rose has had the gift of prophecy most of her life and has found ways to cope with the flashes of foresight that plague her. Jeff has only had the ability for a few months and he needs Rose's help to harness it. He sees her in his future, and puts his plan into action, knowing that an enemy is coming for them both.

An explosive situation, and a dangerous man...

Jeff is tall, sexy and has an air of mystery about him. She doesn't need her prophetic gifts to know that spells trouble. Of course, he's just the sort of trouble she's been craving in her life. When he shows up at her workplace, she agrees to meet him for coffee, but when bad guys start shooting up the local mall to get to them, she follows her instincts and takes the escape he offers...straight into his waiting arms.

A secret base, and a secret unit...

Rose discovers all sorts of things she had never dreamed of before. Whisked away, under fire, to a secret military base, she's offered a job where she's supposed to help Jeff learn more about his newly acquired gift. But, when the enemy attacks the island base, she wonders if she's there to help Jeff, or is it really the other way around? Either way, she discovers a deep and dangerous love for the soldier who stole her heart almost at first sight. Can they fight through to a place where their love can blossom, or are they doomed even before they start? Even Rose can't see that future...

DEDICATION

To all the fans of this series who waited so long for a follow up. Thank you for sticking with me through all the publisher ups and downs and upheavals in my own life. This story had been planned for a very long time. I'm glad I finally got the chance to tell it.

PROLOGUE

Rose came back to the present with a start. She set to work right away, texting her afternoon appointments, telling them she had to cancel. She wasn't sure why, exactly, she wouldn't be available, but it had something to do with a handsome man with a British accent and an aura of danger. Her own personal Mr. Bond.

He was coming for her today, and whatever happened, it was important to her future—to her continued existence—that she at least listen to what he had to say. She was alone in the shop this morning, but she usually locked up when she went to lunch and the owner would be in this afternoon, so even if Rose didn't come back after lunch, it wouldn't matter.

She went about her tasks with her head halfway in the clouds, wondering what the disjointed images she'd seen in her most recent vision meant. There were guns, which made her shiver, and lots of very serious men carrying them. The ones she saw in her mind's eye had a markedly protective feeling to them, but there were others. Ones she couldn't see clearly. Ones who carried the red and black aura of danger.

Danger meant for her? Or, maybe for the protective men? For the hunky Brit? All of the above? She couldn't be sure.

She'd have to wait to find out, but she knew that wouldn't be long. Any minute now, the handsome secret agent guy would walk into the shop and the future would begin to unfold…as she had foreseen.

CHAPTER ONE

Jeff Penworthy, half-British by birth, American Spec Ops warrior by choice, and gifted with visions of the future by some odd twist of Fate, stepped into the small storefront and looked around. It was a psychic shop, one that had become increasingly popular in recent months, though the real attraction was not the frivolous scarves, herbal concoctions and perfumed oils sold behind the small counter. No, the real attraction was the woman who worked there.

She had started working at the shop just a few months ago, doing readings in the back room, using her psychic gifts—along with some moderate showmanship, he was sure—to look into the future. Whether she actually saw the future was of far less importance than the hope she gave to her clients. They were more than willing to drop large sums of money into her lap for the privilege of a reading, but everything he'd been able to find out about the mysterious "Madam Pythia" told him she only accepted a moderate fee from those who sought her out and put in long hours at the shop, trying to make her own ends meet.

Plus, Jeff had the advantage of having seen this woman—or at least a representation of her—in his own psychic visions of the future. For the past few days, the visions had been coming fierce and hot, demanding action on his part. Never had such strong visions overtaken him, and never with the ringing call to action that stirred his warrior's soul.

Trouble swarmed around Madam Pythia, and only Jeff, specialist warrior that he was, could hope to save her. But hunters followed his every step, and those who hunted him and his comrades without success had turned their sights on this innocent woman for reasons known only to themselves. Jeff knew at least that much from his confusing visions. Now, it fell to him to convince the woman of the very real danger coming for her. He also had to make them both believe he could somehow protect her.

He had no idea how, but he would do it, nonetheless. Duty drove him, as did his vow to protect the innocent. It was his sacred honor.

Rose heard the bell above the door tinkle and swallowed the last of her coffee. The heavy tread of the newcomer's boots gave her a small start. Manly steps, she thought, straightening her scarf in the back room before entering the small shop. Women were the usual clientele of the Sacred Way Psychic Shop. Women and just a few men with troubles and lost souls, usually. Not the sure, heavy, booted strides that covered the ground from door to counter in mere moments. Could it be her mystery man had arrived?

"Welcome." She spoke as she walked, shock catching her up short with her first full look at the newcomer. Hard muscles on an even harder frame faced her, with intense, nearly glowing eyes focused on her. A shiver traced down her spine, but it was more than fear. It was awareness.

It was him. And he was so much more than the fuzzy image she had seen in her vision. This man spoke to her senses on so many levels. His dark blue eyes communicated with her soul, his sculpted body enticed her, and his clean, manly scent stirred passions long forgotten. Danger surrounded him, but not for her. No, for her, his body language spoke of protection and safety. It was a contradiction that could be confusing, but his gaze continued to draw her in, even as her footsteps stopped short.

"Madam Pythia?" His strange eyes said he already knew who she was.

Rose nodded. "How can I help you? Are you here for a reading?"

"No, ma'am." His chin was so firm, she thought absently, his slight smile so engaging.

5

"But I have come to speak with you. I can pay you for your time, if need be."

She grew even more intrigued. "I only charge for readings, and I don't have any scheduled for the rest of the day. I can spare you a few minutes."

She knew she had to speak to him. Usually, she kept a reasonable distance from the visitors to the shop, unless they were there for a reading. It's not that she didn't like people, but sometimes, her gift made it hard to be around them. She couldn't always control what she saw and when, making small talk difficult.

"What I have to say may be hard to hear." He seemed to search for words. "Danger follows me to your door." His words were stilted as if he fought to find the right ones. "There are men coming for you. They mean to watch you—perhaps abduct you as a means to get to me."

Fear raced into her heart. "Why? I don't even know you." But she knew the men he was talking about. Not personally, of course, but she'd seen them in her vision. Dark, menacing shadows, following her. Meaning her harm.

"You're in danger. If you have any true gift at all, surely you must have seen this."

The man's denim blue eyes sparkled at her, and for a moment, she could almost swear she saw them glow. Something deep down inside her flared to life, and fear of a different kind threatened to choke her.

"Who are you?"

His stare pinned her. "You know me."

His voice was a gruff rumble, but his words struck her very soul. Somehow...she did know this strange man, this warrior with the wicked blue eyes. More than from this morning's brief vision. The place inside where her gift came from told her of his seriousness. He was the protector her mother had always claimed would come in Rose's time of need. He was her warrior, the one who would be either her salvation or her doom.

The tension of fear left in a rush of air, to be replaced with a new kind of tension as she breathed in his clean, slightly musky scent. The man radiated testosterone, power and energy. His firm jaw alone said he was not a man to be trifled with.

"What's your name?" She wanted so much to know who this startling man was.

He gave a slight shake of his head. "Not here." His eyes closed briefly, and then, that laser gaze was on her again. "Look, is there somewhere we can go? They haven't set surveillance around here yet, but it's coming. Later today, I think. It would be bad for you if they saw me here, but I needed to tell you what I've seen."

The implications of his words stunned her. She'd never met anyone else besides her mother who shared the gift. She knew others must exist somewhere, but her path had never crossed any. Perhaps, until now.

"It'll have to be someplace public. Regardless of my instincts, I don't really know you." She challenged him with her eyes and a firm stance. She trusted her gut and her vision, but she'd be a fool to be alone with this scary man who wouldn't even give her his name.

"A wise precaution." He nodded briefly, and she felt unreasonably glad he thought she was wise. "How about the mall? There's a small café in there that ought to do."

She shot a look at the wall clock. "I'm due for a lunch break. I'll meet you there."

"You go first. I'll follow behind you. This way, you'll know where I am, and I'll know you're safe."

She thought about the path to the nearby mall and nodded. His plan made sense. The route was very public, with little opportunity for him to harm her without someone noticing, if he were so inclined. They went out the door together and then parted after she locked up— each to their own vehicle. She wasn't surprised to find he was driving a big black SUV. He could probably drive right over her little compact car, if he wanted. The thought wasn't comforting, but he maintained a decent distance between their cars on the way to the mall, and when they arrived, he parked a couple of rows over from her, giving her space.

They walked into the mall separately, though she was aware of him always a dozen yards behind her. She walked confidently to the small eatery and asked the hostess for a booth. He was much closer now, and joined Rose at the hostess station without comment.

They slid into a small booth at the back of the café a minute later. True to his word, he hadn't crowded her, only following behind at a respectful distance. Oddly, his presence had made her feel safe in ways she had never felt before.

"So, who are you?" The words left her mouth only moments after the waitress left the table with their order.

"My name is Jeff Penworthy. I'm a lieutenant in the U.S. Army."

"Special Forces." The words left her mouth without her permission, but he didn't seem surprised. His eyes sparkled a deeper blue as his lips quirked up in amusement.

"So, you do have the gift." He sat back, eyeing her.

"Maybe it was a lucky guess."

"You make your living reading the future and making people believe you're psychic. Why would you want me to believe you're not?"

She sat back as well, regarding him from calculating eyes. "Maybe I'm a fraud. Isn't that what you're thinking?"

"Not anymore. You have at least some portion of the gift, or you wouldn't be in danger."

"Yeah, about that—"

Her words were cut off by the arrival of the waitress with their order. It took the woman a few moments to transfer the plates and glasses from her tray to the table, while silence reigned. As soon as she was gone, Jeff spoke.

"I have a strong precognitive gift. It's newly developed and can be damned inconvenient, but it's proven right, time and again. For the past few days, I've been seeing you. Danger surrounds you, from the same source that has been trying to take down me and my friends for the past few weeks. I don't know why they targeted you, but they have. The danger is very real."

"You saw me?" The floor had just dropped out from under Rose, but Jeff's words rang with truth. It was a little side benefit of her psychic gifts—she could always tell when someone was lying. This Jeff Penworthy spoke the truth as he knew it, and that scared her witless.

"At first, I saw the shop. Later, I saw you in the shop and then the watchers. They've had surveillance on you, off and on, for a few weeks now." He took a huge bite out of his sandwich and chewed efficiently, swallowing before he continued. "I figure they started watching you about the same time my team leader and his new wife were kidnapped."

"Are they okay?"

"They broke free, but it was a tough escape. They're safe now, but being careful. Our movements are restricted. All the members of my unit are in danger, and we don't go out alone." His eyes shifted casually to several big men sitting in various locations around the small shop.

Gasping, she realized they were surrounded by men who could only be his unit members. The protective men she'd seen in her vision. She tried not to stare but caught more than one amused glance from the muscle-bound men sipping coffee all around.

"Calm down." A large hand covered hers, sparking electrically between them. "They're here for our protection, not for any nefarious reason."

"How can I trust you?" The words were a broken whisper. His fingers tightened for a moment over hers before letting go as he sat back. She wanted to be brave and follow her vision, but when push came to shove, she was scared of what might happen. This felt big. Bigger than anything she'd ever faced in her comparatively quiet life before.

"How can you not trust me?" he countered, and she knew he was right.

She'd seen this. She'd seen him, and his friends. And she'd seen the dark menacing ones who were coming. All in all, she was better off with him. She knew this from the vision. It had come to prepare her to take a leap of faith. Now, she just had to follow through, despite the fear.

Sighing, she sat back, defeated. "I've never met anyone else who could see the future, besides my mother, that is. She had a powerful gift, but since her passing it's hard for me to see much of anything about my own life with certainty, and never on demand. Things come to me. They bombard me at times, and it's hard to deal with. Is it like that for you?"

"It was at first. I've only had this ability for a few months, but in that time, I've learned ways to control it to a certain extent. At least enough to make it easier to be around people and out in public. Enough to be able to do my job."

"You said you're in the army, but you're not entirely American. You have more than a little accent there." Truth be told, his hint of a British accent was damned sexy.

"My mum is British, but I was born in Florida. She got custody when my folks split up, and I was raised mostly in Surrey. I visited my dad, of course, a couple times a year. He was a Green Beret, and after college, I joined up to follow in the old man's footsteps." He leaned back. "So now, you know all about me. Won't you even tell me your real name?"

She considered for a moment. "Athena Rose Kitsapolous."

"You're kidding." His incredible eyes sparked with humor, inviting her to join in.

"Afraid not."

"What did your mum call you?"

She hesitated. "Rosie." Her mother had been the only person to call her that.

Satisfaction filled his smile. "Sweet Rosie. It suits you."

One moment, Jeff was smiling at the gorgeous woman sitting across from him in the booth, the next, a vision overtook him, sending his inner eye far, far away. The realm was a familiar one, filled with violence and death. A man stalked forward, the glint of blue-black in his hand sending chills through Jeff's body. The gun was for Rosie, he knew that without being told.

Jeff paid attention to what he could see of

the surroundings. He'd learned this trick through harsh trial and error since being given this questionable gift. The surroundings in his vision could tell him the place and might even give him the time. This scene had a feel of urgency to it as well, which he'd learned boded ill. It could mean the events he saw were only moments into the future. Whether he could prevent catastrophe in so short a time was doubtful at best, but he had to try. He always had to try.

The gunman was in the mall, heading for them.

Snapping out of the vision, Jeff sent a series of hand signals to the big men stationed at tables and booths around the room. Instantly, they were on their feet. Jeff stood as he tossed a twenty from his pocket onto the table. It would more than cover the cost of their half-eaten meal.

"We have to go."

"What is it?"

He touched her shoulder, reaching downward to scoop her little hand into his own. As gently as he could, he tugged her up.

"Danger has found us. We have to go. Now."

"You saw it?"

"Just now. A man with a gun, in the mall."

Jeff breathed a sigh of relief when she stopped questioning him and started moving. He needed her cooperation if they were to avoid a potentially deadly scene in the middle of the crowded mall.

He gave the rest of the team a couple more hand signals they all knew so well, and within moments, they were all on the move. Money was left on tables for the wait staff with enough to cover their food and coffee, plus generous tips all around. There would be no complaints about so many tables emptying out so quickly.

Two of his teammates walked out of the café ahead of Jeff and Rosie, two behind, and a few scattered into the environment of the mall as they moved. They didn't look like they were together, but if anyone came close, they would form up around Rosie and protect her—as would Jeff.

Jeff got a flash of insight. "Tango left," he said, just loud enough for the men in front and behind to hear. "Ten o'clock, fifty meters."

"What?" Rosie asked, adorably confused.

"The bad guy is to our left, about fifty meters away. That's why we're cutting down here," Jeff said, taking an abrupt turn down a side corridor of the megamall.

He had more options available. If pursuit continued, there were a multitude of stores they could dive into and go from there into the back areas of the mall. The loading docks and hidden roadways behind and underneath the public areas. It might not smell great down there, but there would be a lot of great places to hide and darkly lit pathways.

Wil dropped back to offer a sit rep. "We're going down to the mall office. Captain's working with the mall cameras and has security on our side. They'll let us into the loading docks and underground roadway from there, and we've got transport on the way."

"Good plan," Jeff replied, then looked at Rosie. Her eyes were wide, and she looked both scared...and skeptical. Damn. He liked that she didn't take anyone on faith, but right now, it was a bit inconvenient. "Rosie—"

The appeal he had been about to make was cut short by the sound of gunfire. Shit!

"Take cover!" one of the guys ordered, and Jeff grabbed Rosie's arm and dragged her behind a kiosk in the center of the mall corridor, along with the frightened kiosk attendant.

A grunt from behind told Jeff that at least one member of their team had been hit, but since there were no urgent calls for a medic, he figured they'd either taken it in the vest or it wasn't a life-threatening wound. Civilians scattered as his teammates yelled at people to get down, hide behind things, or run, depending on their position.

Return fire hadn't really been on the agenda for today, though every member of the team was armed. Still, they weren't quite authorized to act on U.S. soil. Luckily, it looked like somebody had called in local law enforcement.

Two uniformed officers entered the mall between Jeff's group and the shooter. Thankfully, they started shooting back when they realized the shooter was actively taking potshots at Jeff's team while they hunkered down behind potted trees, advertising displays, and shop kiosks in the center of the mall.

The visions were coming in flashes of insight, as they often did when Jeff was in combat situations. They'd trained this particular skill, in simulation, after it had first appeared while they were still in the Middle East. It felt almost natural for him to communicate a safe path for his teammates using the hand signals all Spec Ops soldiers knew. He spared a moment to take Rosie's hand and look into her eyes.

She was scared. Damn. Her eyes were wide with fear, which he hated to see, but at least he knew he could do something about it. He squeezed her hand.

"I know a safe way out. Are you ready to jog?" He looked at her feet, glad to see she'd worn sensible, flat, rubber-soled shoes. They wouldn't hamper her mobility.

"Yes," she gasped as more gunfire erupted nearby. Jeff looked at the kiosk attendant. He'd take her with them if he could. There were too many bullets flying around out here in the middle of the mall passageway.

"Are you coming?" he asked the frightened woman. "We're going to run for better cover."

The woman looked down at her right foot and grimaced. "I'm not running anywhere. Sorry."

Jeff followed her gaze and realized the long, flowing skirt she wore hid a heavy cast on her foot. Yeah, she wouldn't be able to keep up. He made a quick decision and sent a hand signal to one of the team.

"Okay. I'm going to send someone over to

you. He's one of the good guys. He'll keep you safe. Just stay behind the cart and keep as low as possible." The woman didn't look nearly as frightened as he'd expected. Rather, she seemed resigned. An odd reaction in a civilian, but he couldn't worry about that now.

"Thanks for trying. Be careful," the woman advised them as she gripped the handrail of the cart and tried to get in a better position.

"What's your name?" Rosie asked the other woman just as Jeff was about to give the signal to move.

"Hannah," the woman answered. "Hannah Sullivan."

"I'm Rose Kitsapolous. We'll see you again. I'm certain of it." Rosie smiled at Hannah, and she seemed to take heart from that small gift of a grin.

"I'll hold you to that, Rose."

Jeff wondered suddenly if Hannah was some kind of veteran. She had a resignation to the situation that seemed unlikely in someone who had never been under fire before. Right now, of course, he had to focus on getting Rosie to safety.

He tugged on her hand when the time was just right, and they lurched to their feet and made a run for it. He was careful to keep Rosie in front of him, using his body to shield her from any stray bullets. He hoped.

CHAPTER TWO

Rose couldn't believe what was happening. She was in the middle of a shootout in the mall with a team of giant men surrounding her. Not to mention Jeff. He was all the protection she really needed, she thought in one dazed corner of her mind that found all of this fascinating instead of scary. It was the same part of her mind that remembered the vision of the morning. Big men, protecting her. So far, so good.

Jeff ran behind her, keeping himself between her and the shooter. He probably didn't realize she noticed that, but she was observant. She also took note of the giant men who had been scattered around the coffee shop and were now flanking them. One had been limping, and his faded black cargo pants looked like they had a darker spot on the side of his thigh. Had he been shot? Grazed? Whatever had happened, he hadn't let it slow him down.

When she had jumped up from behind the kiosk with Jeff, the wounded fellow had taken their place behind the kiosk, with Hannah. Rose wasn't certain, but her mind was ticklish in the way that she had come to realize meant there was something in the future for that couple. The injured guy and Hannah. Yes, there might be something there, but this was no time to examine the possibilities.

Jeff herded her toward a side door that had a placard over it saying that it was for Authorized Personnel Only. Rose went right in, noting the difference between this no-nonsense maintenance corridor and the fancier parts of the mall. There were scuff marks on the wall from where carts and machines had rubbed the paint away.

They turned a few corners then went down a flight of stairs. The gunfire had ceased above them, but Rose still felt the sense of urgency about getting away from whatever was going on up top. Jeff led the way through a door to the lower level. When he signaled for her to come through, she realized two men were already there, waiting for them. One wore a mall security uniform, and one was definitely one of Jeff's friends. She could tell from the man's sheer size and command presence.

She had a flash of insight and saw the big man in the black T-shirt stopping a car with his bare hands on a dark and rainy night. The harsh set of his features was highlighted in the headlights. Then, she saw him in a sandy place, wearing combat fatigues and captain's bars, if she wasn't mistaken. He was heavily armed and helmeted, but she saw his face clearly, and he was talking to an elaborately dressed man wearing a turban. The turbaned man turned to her in the vision and looked straight at her, smiling before he winked, and the vision disappeared as suddenly as it had come.

Rose gasped. It was like...the man in the turban had seen her watching in the vision, and been amused by it and, somehow, controlled the vision and ended it with that little wink. That had never happened before, and it would have freaked her out if there'd been time to freak out any more just then. As it was, she followed the two men with Jeff at her side and a few of the others following behind. The mall security man unlocked doors for them, using both his big ring of keys and his security pass, until they were in an underground loading dock area.

Three giant black vehicles pulled up as they walked out onto the pavement. Jeff escorted her to the first one, seating her in the passenger seat before going around to the driver's door and taking over from the man who'd driven the vehicle into the underground area. The former driver got into the backseat and buckled in.

"Put that seatbelt on, ma'am. Jeeves doesn't mess around when he drives. You might want to hang onto your hat," the other man said with an unmistakably eager grin. "I'm Dan, by the way."

"Rose," she said, buckling her seatbelt and wondering if she'd just fallen down a rabbit hole, like Alice in Wonderland. Only, her new fantasy world was populated by impossibly huge men with an obvious thirst for adventure.

Jeff spared a glance to make sure she was buckled in before hitting the accelerator. The other two big black vehicles were with him. They formed a small line as they headed out of the underground. Dan had a walkie-talkie and was exchanging coded messages with the men in the other vehicles. One pulled in front of them, and one was behind. They made a conspicuous little parade, she thought, as they drove toward a ramp where she could see sunlight at the top.

"Won't a line of identical black SUVs be noticed?" she asked, her thoughts spilling out of her mouth before she could censor them.

Jeff grinned at her. "Decoys," was all he said, but she understood. His gaze refocused on the ramp and the cautious approach the first car was making. When it hit the top, it paused, as if to draw any possible fire, then sped off.

Jeff didn't pause, and neither did the vehicle behind them. They sped out of the underground and peeled off, each heading in a different direction as soon as they came to a turning point on the looping road that surrounded the giant mall. They didn't present a line of three identical vehicles. They were just solo cars going off and doing their thing. Much less conspicuous. But also, a bit more vulnerable. Rose tried her best to stay calm. Panicking wouldn't help matters.

An image flashed in her mind. "Why am I seeing helicopters?"

She looked at Jeff, and he was smiling. "What did I tell you, Dan? She's got the gift."

"Well, we already knew that based on her file," Dan replied casually.

"File? What file? I have a file?" She demanded of the grinning fool in the backseat. Just what was going on here? "If you're going to abduct me, you're going to have a hell of a time. I fight back."

"It's not abduction." Dan looked insulted.

"It's more like protective custody," Jeff insisted from the driver's seat. "I'm sorry, sweetheart. My actions probably caused the enemy to move up their timeline. They've been watching you for a while, and they know your routine, where you live, where you shop. It's either they grab you or we do. Of the two, we're safer for you."

"Much safer," Dan put in. "We're the good guys."

She wasn't so sure about that despite her earlier vision. She was scared and panic was starting to get the better of her. "Where are you taking me?"

"Well, you can't go home right now," Jeff said, taking a turn much faster than she ever would have. Her body pulled on the safety belt, and she was glad she'd buckled in. "The only truly safe place is with us, and we're currently stationed just off the coast."

"On a ship?" she asked, her voice rising. They had a ship on which a helicopter could land? That image of the helicopter had been so strong. She knew it was in her immediate future.

"An island," Dan piped up from the backseat. "A first-class top-secret military installation."

"The U.S. military?" She wanted to be sure.

Dan looked affronted. "Of course. Who did you think we were?"

"Just checking," she quipped back, more interested in the speeds at which Jeff was driving.

He wasn't dangerous—exactly—but he was going a lot faster than she liked. It was both a little frightening and kind of exhilarating. She'd never really driven with an expert before, and it was clear Jeff was just that—an expert at handling this vehicle, and probably anything else with four wheels and a steering column. He looked every inch the calm professional, even as he raced down the road, dodging traffic and taking turns at a breakneck pace.

The radio squawked, and Dan replied in code. "The closest helipad is compromised," he reported to Jeff.

"Heading for secondary," he responded, and Dan said something into the mic, acknowledging the change.

But they never made it to the secondary site. Pursuit found them even before they got there. What followed was the most harrowing, yet amazing ride of her life. Jeff drove like no one she'd ever seen before in real life. Oh, she'd caught part of a movie about a baby-faced getaway driver a few months ago where the kid kept totally calm, even as he did stunts with his car that she'd though couldn't possibly happen in real life.

She'd been wrong.

Jeff was just as calm and stoic, and he made that SUV do things she never would have believed if she hadn't seen it herself. They were being pursued by two cars, and Jeff allowed it for a bit, but when the men in one of the vehicles started shooting, Jeff pulled a maneuver that caused that car to spin out of control and hit a tree. She wasn't sure exactly what Jeff had done, or what opportunity he'd seen because she only had her limited perspective from the passenger seat, but it certainly looked like he had everything under control.

The remaining car kept after them, but Jeff seemed only to be waiting for the perfect spot. He touched the wheel, sending the SUV in another direction, then stepped on the brakes, demanding a lot from the big vehicle, and receiving it. The other car went speeding past, burning rubber as it overshot the turn Jeff made.

A series of quick turns left her dizzy, and left their pursuit in the dust. A few minutes later, it was clear they'd lost the other car and were driving merrily down the highway toward some other destination.

"Hot damn," Dan said from the backseat.

He was watching out the back window, but there was nothing to see. "Nice driving, Jeeves. You totally lost them." Then, Dan spoke into the radio, as he'd been doing all along, giving the rest of their unit updates. "Heading for the big H," he finished with, making Rose wonder what he was talking about.

"We prepared for this mission by learning all the helipads in the area that could accommodate our choppers," Jeff said offhandedly as he continued to drive. "There's a hospital that has a large enough roof near the shore, which is ideal, since if we're out over the water, we can see any potential problems long before they become big problems." He turned the wheel, taking them onto a side road. "We'll fly over water, up the south shore of the island to our destination. We'll be there in an hour or so."

He sounded so confident.

"Do you use your gift when you do things like this?" She was intrigued by the idea. She'd never had that fine of a control over her own talent.

Jeff shrugged. "Sometimes. I was a good driver before, but now, I can occasionally see the action before it happens."

She got a flash then, of Jeff driving a big army truck with sand in the distance, and he was dressed in desert camouflage. He smiled at her in the vision, and it winked out. She wasn't sure if he'd been smiling at her—the way that turbaned guy in the other vision had—or maybe in the vision he'd been smiling at whoever was sitting in the passenger seat. For sure, it was a vision of the past. Her gift worked both ways. It showed her glimpses of the future, but also, once in a while, of the past.

"You were in a desert. Driving a truck bigger than this. Wearing all brown and tan colors, with sand all around," she said, her mouth reporting what her mind's eye had seen.

A long whistle from the backseat drew her attention. "You see the past, ma'am?"

She nodded at Dan over her shoulder. "Sometimes. I saw a guy in a turban sitting cross-legged in a tower, too. And I think he saw me."

"What makes you say that?" Jeff asked, his eyes narrowing when he glanced at her.

"He winked at me and ended my vision. At least...that's how it felt. I can't be sure. It was weird." She shook her head. She'd grown used to just blurting out whatever she saw during her stint as a paid psychic. Maybe she shouldn't have told them, but it felt good to share her concern about that weirdness.

"Damn," was Dan's only comment.

"There was a guy in a turban," Jeff confirmed, "but it's too much to explain right now. Hang on," he warned a split second before he took a hard left turn and then crossed over traffic to dive into an underground parking structure.

He drove to an elevator shaft, and Dan got out of the car first. He punched the button for the elevator, all the while looking around the garage. They were on the lowest level, where there was little traffic, even though the upper levels had been filled with people and cars heading to and from the hospital.

When the elevator car arrived, Dan stepped inside for a moment, and Rose noticed a small flash of silver in his hand. A key of some sort? He stepped back out again, holding the doors open with his foot while one hand was on his weapon and the other signaled to Jeff, who was still behind the wheel of the running vehicle.

"Wait there, I'm coming around to get you," he said, putting the SUV in park and getting out.

The motor was still running. Rose unclipped her seatbelt, figuring it was go time, and waited impatiently for Jeff to do his own walk around the vehicle, his head on a pivot as he looked around the mostly empty garage.

He came to her door and opened it. She slid down from the high seat, her body brushing up against his, he stood so close. At another time, she would have been exhilarated by the close body contact with handsome Jeff—and she did feel a little flutter in her tummy when she invaded his personal space—but this was no time to have the hots for the hunky soldier who was still in the process of saving her from unknown gunmen.

She scolded herself, and her hormones, back in line. When he held out his hand to her, she took it, steadfastly ignoring the little zap of electricity that seemed to go from him right up her arm to make her entire body tingle. Yowza.

He had her walk in front of him as he

crowded her toward the elevator, leaving the SUV running and in the middle of the roadway nearest the elevator. It offered some protection from anyone trying to shoot at them from the greater part of the garage, but no shots came as they walked the short distance to the open elevator door at a rapid clip.

She stepped into the car and noticed that Dan had inserted a small silver key into the control panel. Some kind of universal override thing? She knew firefighters had some way to control elevators in the city, but she'd never seen it in person. Maybe Dan had the same sort of thing.

"This thing have roof access?" Jeff asked Dan the moment the elevator doors closed.

"No, but it'll take us to the top, and then, it's just a short walk down a maintenance corridor to the stairs. One flight up, and we're in the sky," Dan answered. "I took care of the cameras in here, too, of course."

"Of course," Jeff answered with a mocking little bow of his head and a grin. These two were actually enjoying themselves! Rose could only shake her head. She wasn't an adrenaline junkie and didn't really understand those who were.

As the elevator rose, Jeff and Dan exchanged a few words. Rose understood about one in every three, but she got the gist that other members of the team would retrieve the SUV and that two were already in position to meet them on the roof.

Who were these men that they could so

easily gain cooperation from mall security and hospital staff? They had to be legit, right? She didn't get any sort of bad feeling about them— quite the contrary. Still, she couldn't help but feel that, as she went along with their plan, either she was making the worst mistake of her life or about to embark on a new adventure that would take her places she never would have dreamed.

She was hoping for the latter.

Jeff didn't sense anything either way about possible danger ahead of them. He had a feeling of pursuit, but it wasn't close enough to cause a problem at present. He'd honed his gifts as best he could over the last few months with the help of his teammates and the specialists they'd brought in to help them figure out what had happened to each of them in that foreign desert.

The elevator dinged as they reached the roof. Jeff tensed for action as the door opened. The captain was there, with Wil, their faces reflecting nothing but the mission. Jeff breathed a tad easier. They weren't scowling, which meant they hadn't encountered any problems on the way to this point. That didn't mean, necessarily, that they were completely out of the woods, but it was a good sign.

"This way." Captain Hal Haliwell took point with Dan following after. Jeff gestured for Rosie to go next. He'd be directly behind her with Wil taking rearguard.

Hal led them to a wide staircase. Jeff knew

there had to be another elevator that would allow the hospital to transport patients who came in by chopper down into the building, but they'd opted for this route when they'd devised this backup plan because the elevator they'd used went all the way down to the lowest level of the parking garage. If they'd gone for the elevator that went directly to the roof, they would have had to change over at some point in the middle of the way up, traipsing through patient corridors and public spaces. Not very discreet.

Hal led the way onto the roof after cautiously opening the door and taking a look out. There was a sheltered area next to the elevator door. It was a cinder block cubby that faced the helipad. There was even a bench along the back wall of the dugout-like structure. Jeff realized it was probably used for protection from the elements for hospital staff awaiting patient arrivals. It would serve them as a fortified place to wait, as well.

Hal spoke into his radio then looked at Rose. "Our ride is almost here, ma'am. How are you holding up?"

"I'm okay," Rosie replied in a thin voice. Jeff could feel her nervousness and anxiety.

"Any reports on pursuit?" Jeff asked, hoping for a report that might put her more at ease.

"They went for Mike's vehicle," Hal informed them. "There was a quick firefight, but everybody's okay. Mike led them to the ocean and used that trick with a pod of dolphins and a very accommodating great white shark."

"No way," Dan piped up. "He got a shark to eat a bad guy?"

"Chew on, at least," Hal replied with a sly grin. "There'll be enough left to question as soon as our side picks him up."

"Local assist, Cap'n?" Dan asked.

"They've been surprisingly helpful," Hal reported. "Long Islanders don't mess around when the word terrorism is mentioned."

"Terrorists are chasing us?" Rosie asked, her voice rising in alarm.

Damn. Jeff hadn't meant to worry her more. He'd hoped she'd take the information that the pursuers had been fooled into following one of the decoys as reassurance. Instead, he'd frightened her more.

"Some of them are from countries, and representing governments, that do support terrorism," Hal explained patiently. "But that doesn't mean the people trying to get us are actually terrorists. It's just the simplest explanation for us to use with the local authorities. The real reason they're after us is more complicated, and top secret."

"Chasing us?" Rosie repeated, putting emphasis on the pronoun. "I thought they were chasing me."

"They are chasing you, Rosie," Jeff said gently, "but it's for the same reason they're after us all. My friends and I have been...affected by something. Something similar to the gift you've had all your life."

"You're all clairvoyant?" she asked with

disbelief in her tone.

Hal shook his head. "No, ma'am. We were all affected in different ways, but it's similar to what you can do. Extrasensory. Paranormal, if you will." He shrugged. "It's complicated, but we'll do our best to explain when we get back to base. For now, just know that we can be your allies, and we'll continue to protect you, if you'll let us."

CHAPTER THREE

Anything Rose might have said would have been drowned out by the sudden arrival of a loud army green helicopter. Dan and another man she'd heard him call Wil, leapt into action, running over to the helicopter and opening the sliding door on the rear compartment.

"Time to go," Jeff said in his clipped British tones.

For a moment, she wondered what he'd say if she refused, but then she realized she was being silly. Jeff hadn't been shooting at her. There really was someone out there looking to hurt or abduct her. If not, this had all been some crazy elaborate ruse, which didn't make much sense, either.

Jeff held out his hand, and she took it. She would go with him, trusting her inner voice, and see where this adventure led. Hopefully, it would take her to safety and a greater understanding of what in the world was going on.

Jeff put her in front of himself with the captain

bringing up the rear as they went to the waiting helicopter. The blades had never stopped turning, just slowed down a bit. She put her foot on the steps leading up to the interior compartment, but Jeff solved her height issue by simply pushing on her back and buttocks to propel her up and into the helicopter.

She was a little shocked by his too-familiar touch on her person, but she really couldn't complain. She was a bit short to manage the leap upward on her own, and he had just been practical. Right? Or was there more to his hand on her fanny than she thought?

And…why did she wish there was? Damn. She hadn't even known the man a full twenty-four hours, and she was halfway to inviting him into her bed…and maybe, into her heart.

It had been far too long since she'd been this attracted to a man. In fact, she realized she'd never been quite this attracted to anyone. It wasn't just the cute British accent, either. Jeff had a noble soul. If she could see his aura, it would be clear and bright. Pure. He had a good heart. She just knew it.

Of course, she also could be deluding herself because he was handsome as sin, as well. Maybe her hormones were finally kicking in and making her see things that weren't really there in his character, but she didn't think so. What she sensed about him—and what he'd already done to prove his intention to help her and keep her safe—spoke for her instincts that said he was a warrior of old values, fighting for what was right and just.

The helicopter lifted off, stealing her breath as she gasped. Jeff squeezed her hand, and she realized her eyes were probably round with terror, but the men around her seemed to take the startling lift-off in stride. They looked like competent professionals—neither anxious nor complacent. They looked both vigilant and calm.

She tried to replicate their expressions but found she could not. She'd never been in a helicopter in her life, and the experience was just too startling to pretend it was commonplace. They zoomed up and out over the neighborhood, zipping away at high speed. Soon, they were out over the Atlantic Ocean because the hospital they'd departed from had been near the south shore of Long Island. She assumed they were traveling parallel to the shore, traveling up the coastline because the visibility of potential threats was much easier over open water. If they'd gone over land, there would be any number of places where enemies could conceal themselves and either spy on their path or shoot at them.

Though, she supposed, they'd have to have special armament to take down a chopper. Something that would travel high enough, for one thing. And something that would have enough punch to cause damage at that height. She'd seen reports on the news about things like rocket propelled grenades. RPGs, she had heard them called. In foreign lands, fighters used such things to take down helicopters, but they were illegal here, so nobody should have them.

Of course, a little thing like a law had seldom stopped people intent on mayhem or death from getting what they wanted—guns or ammunition or whatever—and using it. If there were people willing to open fire in the middle of a crowded mall, they were probably willing to get and use illegal weapons.

She saw that grim understanding on the faces of the men who were protecting her. They had dealt with this enemy before. They knew what this enemy was capable of doing. She read vigilance and resignation on their faces. They were prepared for whatever might come their way, and she felt safe with them. Especially with Jeff.

They couldn't really talk over the noise of the

helicopter, but that was okay. She needed a little time to think and she was, oddly enough, enjoying her first experience of being in a helicopter. It wasn't a luxury model, to be sure, but it was fascinating to her. She looked all around with curiosity, noting the various equipment and trying to figure out what everything was meant to do.

Suddenly, the helicopter dove and swung wildly to the left, toward shore. Out of the corner of her eye, she saw something streaking toward them, but then, it was left behind. Someone was shooting at them!

From a boat? It had to be. Her field of view was limited by her position and the walls of the compartment, but she definitely noticed when Wil calmly shouldered a long weapon with an enormous barrel and pointed it out the hatch. He took aim and fired.

The noise was momentarily deafening, but Rose could see the payload—whatever it had been—making a smoky trail down toward the water and then, a moment later, a fiery explosion. Whoever was on that boat probably wouldn't be giving them any further trouble today. She hoped.

She wondered how their actions would be explained if anyone happened to see what had just happened, but that was above her pay grade. Long Island waters were generally crowded, but they were probably far enough offshore that few, if anybody, had seen exactly what had happened.

Wil handed the long-barreled weapon to Jeff, who handled it like a pro. He might seem handsome and urbane, but he was every inch the soldier right now, with that deadly weapon in his hands. Jeff positioned himself by the open hatch while Wil reached upward with one hand to grab on to an overhead support while he closed his eyes and used his other hand to gesture forward, out the open hatch, like he was trying to touch the distant clouds.

A few seconds later, she realized the clouds weren't quite so distant anymore. In fact, there was a cushion of cloud around them, blocking their view—and more importantly, blocking anyone seeing them from below. Had Wil done that? If so, how in the world...?

Maybe it was just a trick of the view or something. She couldn't see all that much out the hatch from her position. Maybe the clouds had been just up ahead of them, and Wil's almost ritualistic motions had nothing to do with the fact that they were now flying through a cloud bank.

Somehow, though... She didn't really think that was the case. Shivers coursed down her spine again. She'd seen some weird stuff today, and this ranked right up there with the rest of the freak show.

Jeff was glad when Wil did his magic trick and called in the cloud cover. Ever since Babylon, every member of the team had some kooky abilities. Wil could control the weather. They just might be able to camouflage their RPG strike as lightning if Thor could just bring the hammer down.

Wil had gone by other nicknames, but now that he had this freaky ability to make it rain, it looked like Thor might just stick. He had argued that his previous call sign—"Ruthless"—was much better, but he was outvoted by the rest of the team.

They could use a little bit of his awakening skills right now, and, in fact, Jeff could see lightning beginning to dance around in the clouds as he looked out the hatch of the helicopter. There had been a line of small boats, each reading hot to their infrared, and their intel partners in the ocean—dolphins of all things—had reported the presence of long, foul-smelling tubes to those who could speak with them. More rocket launchers.

Wil had a line of targets already in his mind, and nothing but a massive thunderstorm would do the trick to both hide them and take out the targets in the way least likely to raise alarms among the civilian population. They'd have to gloss over that first boat with the locals, but considering three others were about to be obliterated by lightning, it probably wouldn't be that difficult.

The hard part was going to be keeping the explosions from the media. Four boats blowing up in the same storm was just a little too much. They'd probably have to report one or two, if there were witnesses, but the others would quietly sink to the bottom of the ocean, taking their secrets with them. They were far enough out to sea that witnesses were unlikely, though the seafaring traffic was greater here than most places along the coast because of the population density. Still, it was manageable. And freak storms that came up out of nowhere were not unheard of.

Any mariner worth his salt, as well as the day-trippers out for some fishing or whale watching, were already headed back to shore. Only the bad guys intent on shooting down their chopper were holding position as the weather intensified. That should make it easier for Wil to hit them with his lightning bolts. It was time for Thor to do his thing.

They were flying a more or less straight path up the south shore of Long Island, quite a distance out to sea so that anyone on shore would not be likely to see them. They would stay out to sea until they got near the forked part at the end of the island, then swerve in toward the land once more, heading for the small island just past Long Island. Plum Island. Made famous by a novel, but known locally as a no man's land, owned and operated by the Federal government.

The story that most people knew said that the

government had sanctioned research into anthrax on Plum Island, but the truth was a bit stranger than fiction. While it was entirely possible that biological research had taken place on the island sometime in the past, its current use was quite different. There was a military base on the island. A very low-key presence that, nevertheless, kept nosy civilians far from the restricted shores of the isolated island.

As soon as they'd returned to the United States, the men of Jeff's unit had been sent there for evaluation. Experts had been quietly flown into New York, and then taken by boat or chopper out to the island, to work with them. Medical doctors, psychiatrists, even experts in extrasensory perception had been found all over the country and brought there under top-secret contracts with the military.

Jeff planned to get Rose in the same way. She needed protection, and he could definitely use her insight into the gift of precognition. She'd had it all her life. He'd only just started. He had no doubt she could teach him things about his gift, and he was going to keep arguing that to the powers-that-be until they agreed to give her an official position as a consultant to the unit. First, though, they had to make it safely to the island.

A great crash of thunder sounded right on top of a blindingly white flash. Jeff shook his head to clear the noise and grinned over at Wil. Good ol' Thor was living up to his new nickname, bringing the hammer down on something almost directly below them. He could see the orange glow through the cloud cover of something burning on the sea below. That was two enemy boats down, two to go.

Another jolt of lightning and thunder rattled the chopper, and a second explosion from beneath the clouds lit the inside of the cabin in an eerie orange glow for a moment. Three down.

Jeff tried to send Rosie a reassuring smile, but she looked half scared to death. White as a sheet and gripping the seat beneath her with a white-knuckled intensity, she nevertheless seemed calm enough. At least on the surface. She was persevering in a difficult situation, and he had to admire her grit.

One more lightning strike—this one at a slightly farther distance, so it didn't shake the chopper quite so much—and they ought to be home free. Jeff didn't relax his stance as the helicopter descended on its path to Plum Island. There could still be more bad guys out there, no matter that his extra senses told him they were in the clear. His clairvoyance was still too new for him to trust it completely. There might be something his gift didn't show him, and that could really trip him up. His best course was to remain prepared, regardless of what his mind's eye might show him.

Maybe, someday, he would be more comfortable with his gift and able to trust it more, but he wasn't there, yet. It just might be that Rosie would be able to help him learn to trust his abilities and discover just how far he could push the envelope. She had so much more experience than he did with clairvoyance. Surely, she must be able to show him things about their shared gift that he hadn't yet fathomed.

He could feel the helicopter making its descent. They were coming in fast to the pad on Plum Island. He kept the rocket launcher ready until they were on the ground, then he turned it over to Dan, who would see to its care and check it into the armory, now that they were back on base. Jeff went to Rosie and helped her release her death grip on the seat.

She was a little unsteady on her feet at first, but he was there to help her out of the chopper and away from the still spinning blades. By the time they were clear, she had regained her equilibrium and was able to walk on her own. She was definitely a trooper, and he found himself liking her even more than he already did.

Dangerous, since he'd sworn off relationships for the time being. His own future was so uncertain, but he did see terrible things happening in the world. Things he had the ability to at least try to stop. Things he had to do in the future to be able to live with himself, even if he failed to stop the tragedies he saw coming.

He wondered if maybe Rosie saw some of those same things. Would she—of all women—be able to understand what drove him to do what he did? He wasn't sure, but if anyone could understand his gift and the lengths to which it was driving him, it would probably be her. If only he could see the outcome of his own future with Rosie, right now... But that wasn't how his gift worked. At least not so far. Maybe she could instruct him better on how to see his own future. Or maybe it was something a seer should never be able to see. He'd pondered that question ever since he'd discovered the ability gifted to him by that strange genie in the desert.

Jeff ushered her into the nearest building. There was a briefing room set up there, where they would be able to talk with the men of his unit. That was the first order of business. No matter how much he wanted to sweep her away from prying eyes and set her up in a comfy nest where she could feel safe after the disturbing events of the day, that would have to wait until at least some of the i's were dotted and t's crossed. Such was life in the military.

"So, where to, now?" Rosie asked, summoning a smile for him that was only a little shaky as they paused just inside the door to the building.

"You need to meet a few people, and then, we can get you settled into a guest room for the night, at least," he told her, trying to sound both jovial and nonchalant. He didn't want to frighten her any more than she had already been frightened.

41

"Lead on, MacDuff," she said. She almost had him believing that she was as eager as she sounded, but he knew it was more than a bit of bluster.

She was holding up well, but her calm world had been turned upside down today. He knew that for a fact. He could see from her wide-eyed reactions that she wasn't much of a daredevil or thrill seeker. She'd done well today, though. He had to give her that. She had guts when it counted, and he admired the heck out of that. Just as he admired her.

Hell, he more than admired her. He was halfway in love with her already. She was smart, brave, kind and beautiful. Everything he'd always wanted and never imagined existing in a woman. Since the team leader, Hal, had gotten hitched, Jeff had been feeling a bit…lonesome…he supposed. Not that he and Hal had been BFFs or anything, but the unit had always done things together.

Now, more often than not, when the rest of the guys were off duty and hanging out, Hal would be off with his new wife, doing couple things. Jeff didn't begrudge Hal that happiness. Not at all. It was more like he was looking from the outside in at a really good relationship, and he wanted that for himself. A woman in his life that could accept him the way he was now. Someone who would stand by him and be there for him, as he would for her.

It was a rare thing to find a soul mate, but if such things really existed, Hal had definitely found his. Jeff thought maybe Rosie might just fit the ticket for himself. Of course, he wasn't altogether certain she would still be speaking to him—let alone anything else—after the ordeal she'd been through today. She could very easily want to wash her hands of all of them, and their crazy situation. He wouldn't blame her in the least. He'd dragged her into this mess—at least, from her point of view.

He could argue that his actions today may have only accelerated the future that he knew was going to come to pass. It wasn't a very strong argument, but she, of all people, would understand the urgency to act on the things he saw coming. He wanted so much to just sit down with her and discuss their shared gift. He had the impression that perhaps her ability, while similar to his, was not exactly the same. He wanted to know more. He wanted to know everything about her. Not just about her mental gifts, but also about the things she liked and disliked. The things that made her smile and the things that gave her joy. He wanted to give her those things.

Jeff knew it was too soon, but something inside him just made him feel as if she was important to him. To his future. To a shared future together.

CHAPTER FOUR

Jeff escorted Rose into what looked like a lounge. A few men were already there, and one woman, who was dressed like a civilian rather than an off-duty military person. The men were wearing the same dark cargo pants Rose had seen before with T-shirts. The bulky webbing vests festooned with equipment were gone, but the men looked no less competent.

The biggest of the group stood up and came forward, the woman at his side. He held out one beefy paw to shake Rose's hand, and she did the polite thing and greeted him again.

"You're the captain, right? Thank you for coming to my aid," she said formally, as they shook hands.

"Captain Haliwell, ma'am. Everybody calls me Hal. And this is my wife, Casey." The big man surprised Rose with the introduction. She hadn't known wives were casually allowed on military bases. Of course, nothing seemed to be normal about this military unit.

Rose exchanged greetings with the captain's wife. She had a warm smile and seemed only a little nervous.

"I heard a bit about your problem today," Casey said, somewhat tentatively. "I hope you're all right."

"Fine, for now," Rose replied with as much of a smile as she could muster. "Thanks to these men." She looked around the room at the small gathering and addressed them all. "I can't thank you all enough for saving me today."

Murmurs and nods of acceptance came from the few men ranged around the room. It was Hal that replied for them all. "We were glad to help. And now, I'm afraid, we—or should I say, one of my team, in particular—needs yours. I assume Jeeves briefed you on his situation?"

By Jeeves, she knew Hal meant Jeff. Apparently, the nickname vibes were strong with this group. She nodded. "He told me some of it, and I will help, if I can, though it still seems a bit hard to believe."

"But you've seen things. You should know better than most that what happened to us—to Jeeves—is real, right?" Hal's words coaxed her into agreement.

"I know such things are real, as you put it. I've dealt with Jeff's particular problem most of my life," she admitted.

Hal smiled. "Good. I'm going to see if we

can get you instated as a consultant to the unit. That would mean a job. Salary. Benefits. That kind of thing. Is that something you would be interested in, at least short-term?"

"Well, I haven't got anything better to do until I'm sure it's safe to go back to my regular life," she admitted, "and I do need to make a living. Nothing changes that. So, if I could get some kind of job here, I would definitely be interested. Thank you." On the one hand, she felt relief, and on the other, panic. "How long do you think I'm going to have to stay here? How long before it's safe for me to live normally again?"

Hal reached up and ran one hand through his short hair as his expression looked troubled. "Honestly, I don't know. You and Jeeves have the best shot of foreseeing that. I know that, as long as you're here, nobody can get to you. Or, to be absolutely clear, they can try, but they won't succeed as long as we're here to protect you. You have my word on that."

"I see," she replied, but really, she didn't see at all. She had little understanding of why her life had been turned upside down. She prayed for clarity, but her gift didn't always work to her command. In fact, it seldom did. She shook her head. "Well, thanks for being honest. I'm not sure what to make of all this."

"You've had a long, stressful day," Casey offered, stepping forward. "Maybe you'd like to see the quarters here. I had the boys make a few changes when I moved in, and I think you'll like the accommodations I had added for us girls."

Rose looked at Jeff, and he just nodded. "Go on. Your bedroom is right next to mine. I'll stop by after the debrief and check on you, okay?"

Rose had no idea how long a debrief might take, but she nodded all the same. She needed some quiet time to process of everything that had happened. Her body was still thrumming along with the chopper blades, and she knew her adrenaline would only hold out a little longer. She wanted to be someplace quiet and private to fall apart, if necessary.

Casey led her down the hall and through a set of double doors to a long corridor that had about ten doors, evenly spaced, running down either side of the corridor. Like a hotel hallway, Rose thought.

"This is the dorm," Casey told her. "Hal and I have the big room up here, close to the outer doors. I think it was meant for the officer in charge or something. There are common bathrooms in the center of the hall, one on either side. I've designated the one on the right for the men and had them help me refit the one on the left for women. See the pink sign? That's so some big brute doesn't get confused in the middle of the night. I refuse to share a bathroom with the entire unit." She wrinkled her nose. "I mean, they're good guys, but they're guys, all the same."

Roes chuckled at Casey's words and the accompanying eye roll as she opened the door with the big pink sign that read LADIES

ONLY. She wasn't sure what she'd expected, but it certainly wasn't the spa-like atmosphere of a room that had obviously been refurbished recently.

A row of toilet stalls on one side couldn't be camouflaged easily, but they had been painted a creamy beige with a subtle pattern overlaid. Probably some kind of stencil, but it was nicely done. The other side of the room had larger compartments. Two were obviously spacious shower stalls, and one larger room at the end had the door open to show a claw-footed soaking tub. Everything was done in neutrals with a sandy, almost beach theme with light pink accents. The effect was both lovely and relaxing.

"Most of the guys are good with their hands," Casey told Rose. "They all helped. One of them did the plumbing changes, and two or three of the others helped with tile, carpentry and fixing the walls. I did the faux finishes on the accent walls, but they all helped paint, too. It was like they were all trying to make me feel welcome."

"That's so sweet," Rose said, just able to picture the big, gruff men helping the petite woman who had married their leader, wanting her to be happy. They really were nice guys, even if they had lethal skills.

"I used to help my big brother flip houses. He would do all the carpentry and heavy repairs, and I would make all the interior decisions about colors, paint and styles. It was fun," Casey admitted, sighing a bit.

"Well, you have a great eye. This is just lovely."

After talking about the décor and the renovation for a few more minutes, Casey suggested Rose take a long hot bath. After the day she'd had, Rose was inclined to agree. Luckily, she didn't have to borrow clean clothes from Casey. The Army apparently had stocked the barracks with plenty of work-out wear in various sizes, and since the men were all size gigantic, the smaller clothing was left for the ladies.

Casey helped her find a set of sweatpants and a T-shirt in one of the supply cabinets, and she was all set for a nice long soak. Casey had gifted her with a spare toiletry set that included fragrant bubble bath and some other niceties. Rose accepted it all gratefully, already thinking about ways she could repay the woman's kindness. She was certain the cherry blossom scented bubble bath hadn't come out of any Army warehouse. The gift set had come from Casey herself.

The generosity of the people Rose had met so far humbled her. Every last man had been willing to put himself in the way of danger to keep her safe, and they'd all been kind and polite when she'd interacted with them later. They had deep bonds with each other, that was much clear. Each had an air about them that was different from most people. And each of the men's energies was slightly different from each other's. Powerful. Dramatic. Almost... magical?

Rose, of all people, knew that this world wasn't always black and white. There were many shades of gray and many things she probably couldn't even imagine that existed alongside the everyday world. Her own gift was proof enough of that. She'd heard rumors about other things—supernatural things—but she hadn't seen anything...until, possibly, today.

There was definitely something different about Jeff and his friends. Something that defied human logic and brushed the realm of the paranormal. While she wasn't exactly afraid of it, she was definitely a little wary. She had no doubts left about Jeff's desire to keep her safe. If he, or any of his friends, had wanted to harm her, there had already been ample opportunity. They were the good guys. She felt certain of that.

What made her wary was what the gifts they had been given were doing to the men, themselves. She well knew that often, there was a price to pay for powers such as the ones she'd already seen in action. Heck, there was a price for her own gift, which she had paid many times over in tears, anguish and guilt when she foresaw something she could not change.

It wasn't easy to see tragedy unfold before your eyes, knowing that if only you could figure out the right thing to do at the right time, in the right place, you might be able to change the outcome. Or not. Even with all her experience, Rose still wasn't sure if some things weren't just meant to be.

Fate. Was it an absolute? She didn't know. For all the things she could see in the future, the answer to that one question was unknowable. At least for her. Maybe someone, somewhere, knew for sure. But who that might be, and where they were, she hadn't a clue.

Rose tried to wipe all of those conflicting thoughts from her mind and sank into a bathtub full of fragrant bubbles. Such luxury wasn't something she indulged in often. After the crazy day she'd had, she was going to enjoy this. A moment of calm in an otherwise chaotic world. Bliss. Made of hot water and bubbles.

*

Rose had just returned to her room and started to settle in when there was a light knock. She went to the door and opened it, not really surprised to find Jeff there.

"I just came to check that you had everything you needed," he told her, his voice pitched low so that it only carried to her. The feeling was intimate, even though the light from the hallway was harsher than the small bedside lamp that was the only illumination she'd left on inside her room.

"Actually, there is one thing you could help me with," she said, seizing on the opportunity to both spend some more time with him and get a hand with something she needed. "Casey said there were spare blankets and pillows on the top shelf of the closet, but even standing on the chair, I can't reach all the way back to snag them. Can you help?" She opened the door wider, inviting him in.

A smile lit his face as he walked directly to the deep closet that had posed such a problem for her. She'd never encountered such a deep shelf before, and the height of it made the entire retrieval process awkward for someone who wasn't at least over six feet tall with a long reach.

"These extended shelves were designed for loaded duffel bags and equipment boxes. We've repurposed a lot of the original designs in these barracks, but there were some things that were just better left alone." He reached up easily and stuck his whole arm into the high space, dragging out a plastic zippered bag that held the promised blankets. Another reach brought out a matching bag that had two pillows inside.

"You're a lifesaver. Thank you."

As she took the bag of pillows from him, their eyes met...and held.

"You know... I mean that in a lot of ways," she added quietly.

"You don't have to thank me. Especially now when my actions might've sped up the inevitable."

"You mean, those guys coming after me?" She tilted her head to one side, trying to understand him. He was a bit more complicated than the other men she knew.

Jeff nodded. "Maybe if I hadn't come to see you so soon, you'd have had more time in your normal life."

She thought about that for a moment, then shook her head slightly. "Or, maybe, they would've come for me at a time when you weren't able to be there to help me. I think, possibly, you pushed up their timetable, which probably meant they weren't as prepared as they would've been otherwise. I think you did the right thing."

He stepped closer, and she let the bag of pillows in her hand fall to her side. "You're very understanding."

"Sometimes, I see future events. You know how that is. It makes you realize that some things are fated and some can be changed by our actions. You changed things for the better in my case. I truly believe that." He was standing so close now, she had to tilt her head up to look into his eyes.

The moment stretched, and the world around them grew quiet with anticipation. Rose could feel that something important was about to happen...maybe.

"I hope you don't think I'm crazy..." He stopped his words with a slight shake of his head and a rueful expression. "Forget I said that. The whole world is crazy for me ever since Iraq." He refocused on her, looking deep into her eyes as his expression grew more serious. "Thing is, I feel something when I'm around you, Rosie. Something almost...electric. When we touch, I feel tingles shoot up my arm." He put actions to his words, placing one big hand on her shoulder.

She felt the tingles he described, radiating

from where his hand rested lightly on her shoulder, reaching down from that point, shooting happily across her skin and into her bloodstream. It was a potent feeling. A positive feeling. Something she'd never felt before with a man, but that she wanted to know more about. A lot more...

"I feel it too," she whispered, needing honesty between them.

A smile lit his eyes from within. "I know this is all happening really fast—"

"Not fast enough," she chided, reaching up to drag his head toward hers. She initiated a kiss that set off an explosion of fireworks in her blood.

Maybe she was being too forward, but it didn't feel like it. Being around Jeff—kissing him—felt like the most natural thing in the world. The more she was with him, the more she wanted to be with him. Not just talking, though that was nice, but in more intimate ways. She wanted to know what it felt like to make love with him.

Crazy as it seemed, she had a real feeling that it wouldn't be just sex with him. No, it would mean something to both of them. How serious they could be, if they gave themselves a chance to find out, she didn't know, but she already felt that Jeff was a significant part of her life. Whether that was just the disruption and drama they'd already been through, which was something she would never forget, or something longer lasting, she had no idea. Only time would tell.

Or...if she was really lucky, she might get a vision that would reassure her about the next step she felt bound and determined to take, but that wasn't likely. Her foretellings were mostly for other people. Seldom did she receive a glimpse of her own future, unless she was somehow involved with the person who starred in her vision.

But she couldn't think about that now. Not when her lips were finally on Jeff's and he was warming to the kiss that she'd wanted for a while. His arms came around her waist, drawing her close. His lips pressed firmly, taking control, his tongue dueling with hers in an incredibly sexy way that made her insides squirm with desire. Jeff certainly knew how to kiss. Hubba hubba.

Smiling at her own thoughts, she kissed him back, running her hands over the muscles that had made her want to touch ever since she'd seen him. He had rock-hard biceps that drew her hands, and his shoulders made her want to grab on and never let go. She could feel the faint ripple of his abs against her as he moved with her toward the bed, but she wanted to see them. She wanted to run her tongue over him and lick him like a lollipop.

She felt the edge of the mattress with the backs of her legs and didn't protest when Jeff lifted her into his arms then placed her down on the bed as if she weighed nothing at all. He was so strong, he made her feel delicate.

When he would have stood, she refused to release him. She locked her fingers together around his neck and tugged him toward her, onto the bed. He didn't resist for long but followed her down onto the mattress, kissing her the whole way, caging her with his much bigger body, his arms on either side of her head, his legs surrounding hers. She felt enveloped in his warmth, and desire shot through her system like wildfire.

He broke the kiss to look deep into her eyes.

"Do you want this?" he asked in a rough voice that sent shivers straight down her spine. "Do you want me?"

She didn't have to think twice. "Yes," she whispered back, lifting up to match her lips to his once more.

Jeff kissed her back with all the enthusiasm she could have hoped for. His kiss stoked the fire that had been burning steadily since the moment he'd walked into the shop. She'd been attracted at first sight, but what she felt had deepened and become bolder as their time together drew on.

They hadn't known each other long in terms of hours and minutes, but in that short time, she felt like she had lived through some of the most stressful moments of her existence. Jeff had been there, at her side. Protecting her. Encouraging her. Seeing her through the tough moments.

They'd lived more than the mere hours together. They'd experienced more than most couples did in months or even years of dating. They'd faced danger together, and she'd learned more about the way he handled a crisis than she had ever expected. That told her a lot about the man. It spoke to his character and the deepest parts of his psyche.

At this moment, she felt she knew Jeff better than any man she had ever been with. Not that there had been many. Her gift made her extremely selective. Too often, she'd meet someone, and a vision would reveal some unseen facet of their lives or character that warned her off. The few men she had been intimate with had all been good guys, but nobody had sparked her fire the way Jeff did just by meeting her gaze. And none had ever been called upon to put himself in danger for her sake.

Jeff hadn't hesitated. He'd waded in and helped free her from an untenable position. He'd saved her life. What she felt was gratitude, yes, but more than that, she felt the undeniable pull of him. As if he was one pole of a magnet and she was the opposite, drawn to him by an invisible, irresistible force.

Not that she wanted to resist. No, Rose was perfectly happy where she was. Thank you very much. The only thing that would make her happier was if there were fewer clothes between her body and his.

As if Jeff heard her silent wish, he lifted away to tug off the T-shirt that kept her from seeing and feeling his incredible upper body. Then, it was her turn as he helped her lift off the borrowed shirt she wore. She was bare beneath it, and he didn't waste any time, his hands going to her breasts, cupping and shaping, learning her curves and what she liked.

His touch was gentle, and the calluses on his hands were just rough enough to remind her that he was a Man with a big, bold, capital *Mmm*.

CHAPTER FIVE

Rose wasn't wearing undies for the simple
fact that she'd had to wash the ones she'd worn
that day, and they were drip-drying in one
corner of the large bathroom. Casey had talked
about getting some supplies for her tomorrow,
but for tonight, Rose was going commando in
her borrowed clothes. Of course, now, it
looked like she wouldn't even need clothes to
sleep in, because she planned to be butt nekkid
with Jeff for as long as he'd stay with her.

She hoped he could stay all night. She had
plans for him. Rose felt herself smile as his
head dipped to nibble his way down over her
collarbone, heading toward her breasts. Yes.
Just what she wanted, right now.

He licked her nipples—first one, then the
other—before closing his mouth over one as

his hand stroked its twin. She had to bite her lip to keep from moaning too loudly. She wasn't sure how soundproof the walls in this building were, and she didn't want everyone to know what they were getting up to. Not on her first night here, at least.

She supposed, if she wanted more with Jeff—and all indications were, at the moment, that she wanted much, much more of this— they would have to figure out whether or not they would go public with his teammates. Since there was talk of getting her some kind of temporary job with the unit, she wasn't sure how that would work. Maybe they'd have to keep things quiet...or maybe not. She supposed they'd cross that bridge when they got to it. For now, she was going to enjoy these moments with Jeff with every fiber of her being.

Something about being shot at earlier in the day made his lovemaking all the more sweet. It wasn't just that, of course. She wasn't that shallow a woman. At least, she hoped she wasn't. But she'd been attracted to Jeff from almost the first moment she'd seen him, and while the shared danger may have accelerated things a lot, she was reasonably certain that, if their relationship had been allowed to develop in the usual way, they still would have ended up in bed together. He was just that...magnetic.

He drew her to him, and she felt almost powerless to resist.

His hands roamed lower, under the loose waistband of her borrowed sweatpants. Going commando had its benefits as his fingers found nothing but skin underneath. He took full advantage, sliding his hands over her hips then lifting her as he cupped her ass, and his strong forearms lowered the waistband of her sweats down, over her hips. She felt the cool air of the room against her heated skin and the warmth of his hands shaping her, stroking her, delving lower and then...between her legs.

Yes.

She kicked her feet to help him take the sweatpants off the rest of the way, and they ended up flying across the room. She didn't care. All she wanted was for them to be gone. Once they were, it was his turn.

She pushed at the waistband of his pants until he got the message. Jeff lifted up and shucked his pants and underwear in a swift move that left her mouth watering. He was built big all over, and she knew with a single glance that she was going to enjoy being ravished by this sexy, sweet man.

His teammates might laugh to hear him described as sweet, but he'd been nothing but kind and understanding to her, except when he'd been being heroic. She admired him so much. She might even be halfway in love with him, if she was being honest with herself, not that she'd tell him that. Not so soon, anyway. She didn't want to scare him off.

Jeff came back to her and took her in his arms. Then, he rolled so that she was on top. Yummy. Just where she wanted to be.

She dragged her body over his, being sure to touch every interesting inch of him with every interested inch of her. His hands gripped her waist and dug in gently a few times when she stroked him. He liked that, she could tell from the way he shivered and tempered his strength.

He was such a good man. She wanted to treat him with all the tenderness she could muster while ravishing him within an inch of his life. Mutually exclusive ideas, usually, but somehow, for them, in this intimate moment, it worked.

"I'm not into waiting," she whispered to him as she lowered her slick pussy over his hardness. Her lips were within a breath of his, and she could swear she saw flames dancing in the backs of his eyes for a heartbeat that stretched out into forever.

"I'm yours, Rosie. Do whatever you want."

With his complete surrender, she felt her feminine power increase. She'd never been given carte blanche by a lover before. She would not abuse the privilege, but she definitely wanted to explore the boundaries...with Jeff. And only with Jeff.

"First time, fast," she told him. "To take the edge off."

"You keep talking like that, I'm going to come, right now," he warned her playfully.

"Then, I'd better get moving," she replied in a saucy tone she'd never used before. It felt right to play with him while they were intimate. More right than anything that had come before with any other man.

She put actions to her words and slid down over him. She wasn't concerned about possible consequences. Casey had confided that all the men had been checked over by a team of doctors when they got back to the States and had been getting regular batteries of tests every week. They all had absolutely clean bills of health, so whatever was going on with them wasn't caused by anything the medical professionals had been able to find. She couldn't catch anything from him.

And, for her part, Rose was on the pill, so she wouldn't get pregnant. She'd had her supply in her pocketbook, which thankfully, had come through the ordeal with her. She had her I.D., some money, mascara, eyeliner, plus a few other cosmetics, her keys, and some other odds and ends, including her pill case.

Those details taken care of, Rose settled over him, taking his hard length into her willing body. Long and thick, he fit all the empty places within her—both physically and somehow…spiritually. It felt as if this wasn't just a joining on the physical plane, but a more esoteric mingling of energy and spirit, as well. She couldn't describe the feeling that flooded into her when they joined for the first time.

It was like some giant gong had been rung in the ether, and the reverberations shook the air around them with silent waves of recognition. Rightness. Unity on a basic level she'd never before experienced.

"Wow."

They both spoke in unison, then their eyes met, and they smiled.

"If that's the beginning, I can't wait to find

out how this ends," Jeff said, gasping a bit as she squirmed to get more comfortable with him inside her.

"All in good time," she teased gently, feeling powerful and ultra-feminine.

She tried to hold back, but once she started moving, she was lost to sensation. The feel of him within her, his warmth beneath her, reaching up to surround her... It was all just a bit too much for her to handle. She rode him hard and then came hard, much too soon. But Jeff was ready. He lifted her and rolled gently, keeping them joined as he took over the rhythm that she had momentarily lost to pleasure.

He stroked her deep and hard, raising her passion once more, to an even higher peak than the first. She came again, crying out his name, not caring who heard, though she had little breath left to make much noise. Jeff was potent and powerful. Commanding and coaxing as he wrung every last drop of pleasure out of her willing body.

This time, he was with her, clutching her hip and shoulder, gripping just a little tighter than he probably should, but she didn't mind in the least. She might have marks later, but she'd wear them proudly. He wasn't really hurting her. She'd just driven him beyond control, and that put a smile of glee on her face, even as he released her and began smoothing his fingers over the slightly abused areas.

"I'm sorry," he said over and over.

She shushed him with gentle motions. "It's okay. I'm okay," she reassured him.

"Are you sure?" he asked, looking deep into her eyes, even as his breathing rasped in and out of his chest. They were both coming down from a height of pleasure, but she was touched by the immediacy of his concern.

"Very sure." She pushed at his shoulder until he collapsed beside her on the bed, then she snuggled into his side and put one hand possessively over his heart. "You rocked my world, my friend."

He laughed out loud and put his hand over hers. "No, sweetheart, you rocked mine."

"Let's agree to mutual rocking of worlds and leave it at that. For now." Her tone promised more rocking of worlds to come, and he didn't disagree.

As they lay there, catching their breath, Jeff stroked her skin and counted himself lucky. He hadn't expected any of this, but he was happier than he had any right to be at the moment, with this lovely, talented woman in his arms.

Thinking about her gift made him wonder. Maybe she would be willing to answer some of his questions now, though he wouldn't push. Her gift was something he wanted to learn much more about, but she had to be willing to discuss it. He wouldn't try to take what she didn't want to give. Still, he was tempted to ask a few basic questions and see how she responded...

"So, how does your gift work?" he asked, figuring his usual boldness was better than pretend timidity. "Are you able to call visions of the future to you when you read your clients at the shop? Or is that just sleight of hand, and your gift is less obedient than that?" Jeff asked, running his fingers idly through her soft hair.

He loved her wavy dark hair. It was just as luxurious as it looked, and he felt privileged to have that intimate knowledge. He never would have expected her to jump into bed with him so quickly, and he sensed she wasn't normally so impetuous, but he was grateful. Even if this was just a knee-jerk reaction to the danger they'd faced earlier, he would do everything in his power to make sure this wasn't a one-time thing.

Something about Rosie called to him on a very basic level. Something compelling. Something that made him want to stake a claim and make her his own...forever.

The thought made him pause, but she was talking, so he didn't have time to focus on the way that last word had made him jolt inwardly. He'd have time to think about the ramifications of his instincts later. For now, he wanted to learn more about their shared gift, and he made himself pay attention.

"When people come to the shop for readings, I use tarot cards and give them the standard information the cards provide. I'd like to think that my innate gifts make my tarot readings a bit more prophetic than if other people do them, but I can't really know that for certain." She shrugged, her soft skin sliding against his where they touched, which was very distracting. "Of course, it does sometimes happen. A tarot reading will spark a vision, and I'll be able to tell someone something I've really seen. Not all the time, of course, but often enough that I've gained a bit of a reputation among the clients at the shop."

"What about before? When you were in that research study?"

She drew back to look up at him. "You know about that?"

"They had to compile a file on you before they would clear me to approach you. I knew you were on the level, but the military had to be sure before they'd extend our protection to you." He shrugged. "I'm sorry. I know it was a bit invasive. There are probably things in your file that should be given, not taken."

"You didn't read the file?" She leaned back to meet his gaze.

"Hal did. That's his job. He just told me about the research study, because he thinks that's the angle he can use to get you listed as a consultant, because of your prior experience and track record there." Jeff rubbed his fingers over her shoulder, trying to offer comfort. "But don't worry about Hal. He's our captain for a reason. He's the man we trust with all our deepest secrets."

"I can hear the admiration and respect in your voice when you speak of him," she said softly. "He must be quite a guy."

"He's had it a little rougher than the rest of us with our new abilities. His is a more...uh...physically demanding gift, and it's been wreaking havoc on his system. I secretly think, when he talked the brass into sending us here, he was coming home to die. He's originally from Long Island, and he's known Casey most of her life. Only recently did they get together, though."

"That's so sad. Can't anyone help him medically?" Rosie frowned.

"Oh, he's stabilized quite a bit since Casey came here. She's really good for him, and one of our guys is a whiz with medical stuff. I think, between the two of them, they'll keep Hal around for a long time to come." Jeff ran his free hand over his hair. He didn't like thinking about how bad off Hal had been before they came back to the States. "I'm happy for him. He's our leader. Our backbone. I'm not sure what we'd all do without him."

"I'm glad he's found happiness." She touched Jeff's arm in a comforting way for a moment, then her fingers tightened.

Rose was hit with a vision as she contemplated the story Jeff had just told her about Hal and Casey. In it, she saw Hal as an old man with white hair, still cut short in the military style she'd seen him sporting earlier. Casey had a bit of gray in her hair, too, and they were standing at a long table in what looked like a cozy home. The places were set for what looked like Thanksgiving dinner, and there were a number of other people there that bore a striking resemblance to Hal and Casey.

Their children? Something about the vision told her that these others were, in fact, Hal and

Casey's kids and their spouses and significant others. The happiness around that table brought a tear to Rose's eye, and she clutched at Jeff's arm.

"What is it?" Jeff sounded alert to any threat, and Rose consciously let go of his arm and patted it reassuringly.

"Don't worry about Hal. I just saw him and Casey and a bunch of their kids as adults, gathering for Thanksgiving." She couldn't keep the teardrop from tracking down the side of her face, but it was a happy tear.

"Seriously?" She could hear the dawning relief in Jeff's tone.

Rose rolled over and lifted up on her forearms so she could look at him face to face. She nodded, smiling. "It was a big house with a long table. Hal's hair was white, and Casey's had a little gray in it. There were..." she counted up the scene mentally, "...at least five couples ranging in age from twenty-something to maybe thirty-something. One half of each couple looked a lot like they were Casey and Hal's kids, and the other half were spouses, girlfriends or boyfriends. I think there was even a stroller in the background and maybe a grandbaby off to one side with one of the older couples. They all looked so happy."

Jeff reached up and wiped away the joyful tear that tracked down her face. "You've given me a great gift," he said solemnly. "I've been worried about Hal. We all have. I'd like to tell the other guys, but I'm not sure how much to reveal."

Rose shook her head slightly. "That's always the tricky part. It's hard to know how much is too much—or not enough."

"You have more experience with this than I do," he said.

She nodded once. "True, but that doesn't really make it any easier. I think, maybe, we just tell the guys that I've seen both Casey and Hal as old folks with a big family. I wouldn't go into detail about how many kids or what they looked like. I think some things should still be a surprise, you know?"

"You are a wise, wise woman," Jeff said, reaching up to kiss her playfully.

When he drew back, she shrugged. "Plus, I can always tell them more later. We'll start off slow and see how it goes."

"Sounds like a good plan, sweetheart. And speaking of good plans…"

He tugged her downward so that she was lying on top of him. Matching her lips to his, he kissed her soundly, and they were lost to the moment…and all the delicious moments that followed.

CHAPTER SIX

In the morning, Rose and Jeff parted at her doorway, each going off in slightly different directions to get ready for their day. As far as the military was concerned, Jeff and his unit were all on active duty, so he had to report, along with the rest of his team, for their usual morning routine.

Rose ran into Casey coming out of the ladies' room, and the other woman gave Rose directions to what she called the mess hall, and a promise to meet there for coffee after Rose was dressed and ready for the day. Casey smiled extra wide but didn't make any comments about Rose's disheveled hair or the slightly abraded bits of skin that were visible above her T-shirt. Rose blushed when she got a look at herself in the bathroom mirror. She had little doubt that

Casey had very accurately guessed what Rose had been up to last night, but she was grateful Casey hadn't teased her about it.

It was still too new to joke about. Her feelings for Jeff weren't fragile, exactly, but they were just starting to fill in. On one hand, it felt like she'd known him forever, but on the other, she was still learning the little things that made him unique in a world full of people. She wanted to hug this time to her heart and hold it close. Time of discovery and fascination. She prayed it would last and that something more long-term might come of it, though she didn't know for certain if that path was open to either one of them, considering their exceptional circumstances.

For now, she vowed to just enjoy the time they had together and let things unfold. If her gift would just allow her a tiny glimpse of the future, it might help, but she knew from long experience that her talent didn't always work like that. When she most wanted a vision was usually when they dried up. Something about putting stress on herself locked down her gift. At least, that's the way it had always seemed.

Rose joined Casey for coffee after a long, hot shower. She discovered her in the big room that contained a coffee station and a buffet table that was fed from the kitchen directly behind. The dining room had a long row of windows looking out onto the beach. Casey was already seated there, watching a row of men in green fatigues going through their exercise routine.

A quick glance proved that Jeff was part of the group, as were the other guys she'd met the day before. They started their day with exercise, and she was just in time to watch the free show while she sipped coffee. The buffet table didn't have any hot dishes on it yet, but there were a couple of steamer pans that looked like they were about ready for business, so she assumed the full breakfast would be served when the men came in after their calisthenics.

"Just in time for the floor show," Casey commented as Rose took a seat across from her at the table that butted up against the windows.

"They do this every morning?" Rose asked.

"Like clockwork, unless they've got a mission or something special on the agenda," Casey told her.

Rose noticed the way Casey's eyes were trained on her man, as if she was worried. She did a good job hiding her anxiety, but Rose saw the little worry lines around her eyes and the taut line of her lips. If Casey's worry was related to Hal's health and longevity, Rose knew she could say something to help ease that concern, but would Casey believe her? Rose knew she had to try, but she chose a cautious approach.

"So...you know about Jeff's...um...ability?" Rose asked, trying to sound nonchalant, but knowing she failed miserably. She wasn't cut out for undercover work, that was certain. She was about as subtle as a sledgehammer sometimes.

Casey looked at her, but answered frankly.

BIANCA D'ARC

"You mean, how he can see the future?"

Rose nodded slowly. "The reason he came to get me—to warn me—is that I've had a bit of that ability pretty much all my life."

"So that's why you're here." Casey looked as if she'd just discovered some missing piece to a puzzle she hadn't known existed. Apparently, Hal hadn't talked about Rose's background to his significant other, which was somewhat comforting. She'd thought everyone knew about her, but apparently, the guys weren't gossips.

"I was working in a new age shop doing tarot card readings when Jeff walked in yesterday. I don't really need the cards if my gift decides to cooperate," she confided. "Thing is, Jeff was telling me about how he was concerned for Hal, and a vision hit me." Casey turned white as a sheet, and Rose was quick to reach out and cover the woman's hands with her own across the table. "It was nothing bad," she rushed to reassure Casey. "In fact, it was exactly the opposite. I saw you both, in a family setting, and you were both a lot older and looking very happy together."

"We were?" Casey's color returned in a rush as Rose's words registered.

Rose sat back, releasing Casey's hands. "I haven't seen anything between now and then for you two yet, so I can't guarantee that life won't have its usual hiccups, but the end game for you both was really good. Hal had white hair, and yours was going a bit gray. You were together. Whole, and very happy."

Casey was silent a moment and seemed to be blinking back tears. Rose politely sipped her coffee, giving Casey a few moments to collect herself.

"That's…amazing. Thank you so much for telling me, Rose. I admit, I've been very concerned about Hal's wellbeing. Especially since we learned that I'm pregnant."

"You are?" Rose hadn't seen that in a vision, but she didn't have control over what was shown to her and what wasn't. "Congratulations."

"Thanks. It's very early days yet. I'm only a few weeks gone, so it'll be a while before it starts to show. Hal's happy and so am I, though I still worry about him," Casey confessed. "I want him to be around to see his baby daughter and help raise her. His new ability… It takes a lot out of him. I've been worried it could cut his life shorter than it should be, and there's no medical precedent to tell us for sure what will happen with any of the guys." She looked back out the window, where the men were now doing pushups. "They've become like family in such a short time. I'd hate for any of them to suffer for what happened to them."

"The turbaned man in the desert," Rose said aloud. "He had something to do with it."

"How did you know that? Did Jeeves tell you about it already?" Casey asked, her eyes narrowing.

Rose shook her head. "I saw it yesterday. I saw the man in the turban. And he saw me, which freaked me out, I can tell you. I've never had that happen in a vision before."

"Hal thinks that man was a djinn. Like a genie," Casey said in a low voice.

"No way," Rose responded in the same hushed tone.

Casey nodded significantly. "There aren't many other ways to explain what happened to them." Casey looked around toward the kitchen opening where a few people could be seen working. "But we probably shouldn't be talking about this here, even though everybody on the island has top-secret clearance."

"I don't," Rose objected.

Casey grinned. "Yours came through before they ever left the base to get you. I know that much. Hal had a file on you that was compiled years ago by some other government agency."

"Seriously?" Rose supposed that had come from the research study she'd participated in, but she'd assumed all records from that had been either destroyed or locked away someplace dark and inaccessible.

"That's all I know, and I probably shouldn't have found out that much, but I walked into Hal's office a couple days ago and saw it in his hands. All I could make out was the name on the cover—yours—and an agency name I didn't recognize on the folder. Hal put it away as soon as I got there, and he scowled in that way he has." Casey's grin widened, and her gaze went soft. "He still hasn't gotten used to having me around. He's so used to being a lone wolf, and I'm okay with that for the most part. I mean, I know his position means that there's a lot I can't ask him. That's fine, but there's no way I'm going to tiptoe around in our own home. If he wants to keep an office in our suite, then he's going to have to get used to me barging in from time to time, right?"

Rose nodded, chuckling along with Casey as she made her point. They sipped coffee and talked about general topics while watching the men finish their workout routine. When they headed back into the building, Casey got up and poked her head into the kitchen. Rose heard her announce to the personnel inside that the PT had wrapped up and the men would be arriving shortly.

"They all hit the showers after PT, but they're fast. They'll start rolling in here in about five or ten minutes, max," Casey told Rose as she returned to the table they'd been sharing.

Sure enough, Hal was the first one to arrive in the mess hall, just as the hot food began appearing in the steam trays. Pancakes, eggs, bacon, sausage, biscuits, muffins and all sorts of condiments were available within moments, and Hal filled two plates. When he joined the women at the table, he put the smaller plate in front of Casey, who thanked him with a loving smile.

Rose stood and excused herself. "I'm going to get some before the others arrive," she told Casey and Hal.

"Good plan. There won't be anything left if you wait too long," Casey advised.

Twenty minutes later, Rose understood what Casey had meant. As much food as had been laid out for the men, it was all gone in short order. Rose had gotten a scoop of scrambled eggs and some bacon, but that was more than she usually ate for breakfast, so it was plenty for her. Still, the amount of food the men packed away was impressive.

More impressive was the fact that not one of them sported any extra weight. They were all ripped and muscular, but none appeared vain in the least. They seemed like a well-balanced group of guys who were friends and co-workers that had bonded into something closer to a large family unit.

It was clear Hal was at the head of the family. He was the older-brother-in-charge, and Casey was everybody's sister. They treated her with respect and good-natured ribbing, just like her man.

As the newcomer among them, Rose felt a little at odds with the group, but they were welcoming, if a bit stand-offish, at first. It was Hal who brought up the subject that made the guys a bit more comfortable around her, when he spoke openly of her gift as they were sitting around sipping coffee after breakfast had been consumed.

"I want you all to know that I've gotten the go-ahead to employ Rose as a consultant to the unit," Hal said when there was a lull in the conversation, garnering everyone's attention. "It turns out she's a real-deal, government-sanctioned psychic. She did a stint with Dr. Holbrook's initial study but wasn't invited to participate in subsequent projects because of her civilian status." Hal turned to Rose and spoke directly to her, though everyone was listening. "Dr. Holbrook was one of the first they brought in when we got back to the States. She's been working with some of us who have abilities she's more or less familiar with. She indicated that you parted on good terms and was glad to know you'd been brought in to help our man, Jeeves, here."

Rose remembered the young researcher. She'd been good to work with and had helped Rose expand her own knowledge of her abilities, but the study had ended, and they'd gone their separate ways. Rose hadn't realized Holbrook had gone on to do more work for the military, but it made sense.

"I liked her," Rose replied to Hal's unspoken question. "She was fair and competent. I'd be happy to see her again."

"Good," Hal said, then put his napkin on the table before he rose. "That's settled." He looked around the table at everyone. "We've got a debrief at eleven hundred. You've all got things to do before then."

The men took that as their cue to get up and bus their trays back toward the kitchen. The hatch between the two rooms had been shut while the men ate, but it reopened now as soon as the first trays hit the stainless-steel surface of the countertop.

Hal remained standing as Casey got up and took their trays over. He seemed to want a moment to talk to Rose, so she waited to see what he wanted.

"Dr. Holbrook is set up in the building next door. I think maybe you should report there after this and get reacquainted. Jeeves can take you." Hal nodded to Jeff, who stood just over her shoulder. "You'll be part of Holbrook's team on paper, but your experience makes you more or less a free agent. I hope you and Holbrook can come to an understanding of how to work together while maintaining your own areas of expertise."

"She was always fair-minded," Rose said with genuine confidence. "I think we'll work well together, but you're right, we should probably hash out areas of responsibility. I take it you want me to work exclusively with Jeff for now?"

"To start," Hal agreed. "They've been able to help him harness a lot of his gift, but there are still rough spots that are probably more about instinct than rote learning. That's where you come in, according to Jeeves and Holbrook."

"Because I've had the gift all my life and learned a lot of it by instinct," she said, nodding. It was amazingly freeing to be able to talk of her gift so openly. Such discussions had been rare in her life—except for the time she'd spent working with Dr. Holbrook years ago.

"If you think you can help some of the others as we go along, that would be great, but let's play it by ear. We're all learning together here, it seems," Hal gave her a smile that put her at ease. He really was a charming giant when he wanted to be. Remembering her vision of his future, she knew he was going to be a great father when the time came.

*

Jeff ushered Rosie to the small building next door to the barracks the unit had more or less taken over since arriving on Plum Island. Luckily, there were a lot of disused buildings that they had been able to put back into service with a bit of elbow grease. The barracks they were living and working out of now had been derelict when they arrived, but the team had used the time they were confined to base to fix it up until it was livable.

They'd stayed in the main housing area with the others stationed on the island at first, but it hadn't been ideal. While everyone on the island had top-secret clearance, that didn't mean they all knew what was going on with the Spec Ops unit that had suddenly descended on them. They all had their own projects to work on, and it was better that the groups not fraternize too much, lest curiosity get the better of someone on either side.

Jeff had liked Dr. Jeana Holbrook. She was a fascinating woman with spooky green eyes, but although he knew she was a beautiful woman, since seeing Rosie in his visions, he'd been ruined for all other women. Nothing could compare with Rosie's deep brown eyes and glossy dark hair. It was as if she'd mesmerized him before they'd even met, and the effect only got stronger the more he was around her.

And after last night... Well, he was thinking very serious thoughts after the night they'd spent together. Committed thoughts. Forever thoughts.

As they walked next door together, Jeff purposely kept their conversation light. He gave her a rundown of the general schedule of life on base and what she could expect, as long as they weren't called out on a mission. Of course, they hadn't been sent on any real away missions since they'd gotten back to the States. The only missions now, were of their own making. Until they neutralized the threat to the team, that was the only kind of missions they were likely to get.

Jeff held the door for Rosie and let her precede him into the designated lab building. A lot of the guys spent a portion of their days over here, working on the gifts that had appeared after their encounter with what Hal believed to be a djinn in the ancient city of Babylon. They'd set up various rooms for each guy's specific issue, if they needed a safe environment in which to practice.

Since Jeff's gift wasn't anything like that, he didn't have a specific place where he practiced. He just tried to be open, as Dr. Holbrook had instructed, and let the magic happen. For the most part, he'd had some success, but he also knew—due to visions of the future he'd received—that he needed Rosie there. Whether it was for her to teach him more about their shared gift, like he'd told the others, or for some other reason, he wasn't altogether certain.

He'd achieved his goal in getting her to the island. Now, he would wait to see how events unfolded. Jeana was waiting just inside the hall when Jeff ushered Rosie inside. The two women smiled, obviously recognizing each other, and Jeana held out her hands in welcome.

Rosie exchanged a warm handclasp and brief hug with the other woman, both talking about how good it was to see each other, once again. Clearly, they had parted on good terms and remembered each other with fondness. Good. That was one hurdle jumped. Jeff hadn't known what he would do if the two ladies couldn't work together.

"I'm so glad you're here," Jeana was saying to Rosie. "I was sorry you couldn't participate in my more recent research. I've missed your predictive accuracy a lot."

Rosie blushed a bit, but Jeff wasn't one to let an interesting point go. "Accuracy?" he prompted the doctor, who nodded, including him in the conversation.

"Rose was the most reliable foreseer I've ever had the good fortune to observe. Until now, that is. It'll be interesting to see how your abilities match up," Jeana said, looking them both up and down as if considering. "Shall we go into my office and figure out how this is going to work?"

CHAPTER SEVEN

Jeana led them into her small office where there was just enough room for them all to sit. They had a casual discussion about Rosie's presence on the island and her area of expertise. Jeff was an observer, for the most part, and was glad to see things between the two women were going to work out well, if this initial meeting was any indication.

Before long, Jeana and Rosie had ironed out the ground rules and agreed to check in with each other at the end of each day of work to see what, if anything, needed adjusting. Rosie was assigned a comfortable office-like room that Jeana told her she was free to decorate however she liked. Jeff volunteered to help her get the room set up to her specifications, and then, Jeana left them to discuss both the modifications to the room and how they might begin their work together, exploring Jeff's precognitive gift.

To start, they moved a few comfortable chairs into the space and added a small round table. Rosie directed him to place the table at the exact center of the small room, with the chairs on opposite sides. Then, she dug into her pocket and came out with a small velvet pouch. Inside, was a sphere of clear glass—or, perhaps, it was crystal—which she took out and rolled in her palm.

"It may be cliché," Rosie said with a self-conscious shrug, "but sometimes, it helps to focus on a crystal ball. This one is clear quartz, and I usually keep it in my pocketbook, like a little talisman. I brought it with me, this morning, to see if maybe it could help you— help us both—focus a bit. Have you tried using crystals before?"

"No," he answered, taking the seat opposite her as she sat down and indicated he should do the same. "I tried meditating on a flame once, but it didn't do much."

"Flames are tricky," she replied. "They can help focus within, but for our gift, I think the trick is to focus on the unseen world outside ourselves. If that makes any sense to you."

"I think I understand," he told her. Heaven knew, he'd had a lot of time to think about this unexpected ability since meeting that turbaned man in ancient Babylon.

She dumped the little velvet pouch out over the table, and a small angled tube of clear plastic rolled out and eventually settled on the table. It was a stand, he realized, that would support the weight of the little crystal ball handily. Rosie set up the small ball, which was only about three inches in diameter and perfectly clear. Then, she put both of her hands on the table, spread out to either side of the ball at its center.

"This'll probably get easier when we've got the mood of this room more under control, but it couldn't hurt to at least show you some of the things my mother taught me as a little girl when my power first started to manifest." Rosie shrugged and closed her eyes, taking a deep breath. "The first thing we need is calm and focus. Meditation helps, so if you're familiar already with it, you're one step ahead of where I was when I first started seeing the future."

"I've studied martial arts since I was a kid," Jeff told her. "Meditation was often a part of it, though I can't profess to be an expert at it, or anything."

Rosie opened her eyes and smiled at him. "This is a no judgment zone. We are just floating through the moment, here, together." She wiggled her fingers invitingly. "Give me your hands."

Jeff complied readily. He loved touching Rosie. Any time. Any place. Any way she wanted. Damn. He felt his erection stir at the thought and sternly told himself to settle down.

Jeff placed his hands in hers and followed when she laced their fingers together then laid their hands on their sides, palms facing the crystal ball at the center of the table. She was so beautiful. He had to catch his breath, realizing he'd seen a flash of this exact moment weeks ago, in a vision.

"I've seen this before," he told her.

"What?" Her gaze narrowed as a soft smile played around the corners of her mouth.

"I saw our hands and this table...and your face. It was the first time I saw your face," he told her. "It was just a flash at the time, but what I saw in that vision intrigued me, and I knew it was something really significant."

Her eyes widened. "That's... Well, it's pretty cool. I hope we can live up to the advance billing," she quipped, making him smile and setting them both at ease.

They sat there for a long moment, smiling and looking into each other's eyes. There was no discomfort. No embarrassment. Not after the intimacies they had shared the night before. It was just the two of them. Together. Sharing space. Holding hands.

"Okay," Rosie said after a few moments. "My mother said to look into the center of the crystal and send your inner eye outward. It's not easy, but with your past meditation practice, it might come easier to you than it did to me." She shrugged. "Ready?"

"Whenever you are," he replied at once.

"Good. Now, look into the crystal's heart." She lowered her eyes and did as she instructed. After a few seconds, he did the same.

And then...everything changed.

Except for the comparatively brief time Rose had spent working with Jeana years ago, and the time she'd spent learning about her gift from her mother, Rose hadn't worked with someone this closely in years. Never had she shared her gift with a man. It was way more intimate than she had expected, but yet, with Jeff, it felt right. So right. Like just about everything they did together. As if another piece of the puzzle of her life had clicked into place.

Just like that.

She clenched his fingers as she was launched into the darkness. It was a vision. Nighttime. The hiss of water. Waves lapping at the shore. Sand. Overcast sky. No moonlight. Darkness shimmering on darkness as the water morphed and turned into black shapes coming closer. Men! Men in scuba gear, walking out of the waves, holding sticks.

Not sticks. Weapons.

"Shit." Jeff's voice came to her from outside the vision but didn't interrupt.

"Are you seeing this?" she whispered, afraid to break the link to whatever or wherever the visions came from.

"If you mean some kind of SEAL team stealthing up the beach loaded for bear, that would be a roger."

She took that as a yes. This was a first. They were seeing the same thing at the same time. Was it because she was holding his hands? But, no. She'd held her mother's hands when visions had hit, and her mother hadn't seen what she had. There had to be some other reason, but what did it matter, right now? This vision was important. Rose sensed it. This was vital to the next few days of their lives here on this island.

"Do you know where this is?" she asked Jeff.

"I think so. See the rock jetty off to the left? There are only two of those on this island, and this is the one by our barracks. Where we do our PT in the morning. See the curvature of the shoreline? That's what gives it away."

"You're good at this. What else can you pick out? While it lasts, see as much as you can from the vision. It won't come any clearer after the fact. You have to note things now, while it's happening."

Following her own advice, she made mental notes on what she was seeing. Jeff had the location. She started counting heads and noting their positions. She didn't know anything about weapons, but she looked at the gear each man was wearing as best she could in the gloom. Then, she looked up and noted the pattern of clouds in the sky. There was a clear spot coming. And a clear spot had just passed over, judging by the movement above. The men had waited for the clouds to come ashore.

She looked around her—first left and then right. She saw nothing else on the beach. Taking a breath for courage, she turned her back on the men now advancing toward her position on the beach. She wasn't really there. They couldn't hurt her. It still made her feel vulnerable to turn her back on what was likely an enemy. She noted the lights in the windows of the barracks and the positions of the buildings.

Jeff was right. They were on the beach she had seen earlier. Where the men did their exercise routine each morning. The barracks were in front of them, and the building they were in, right now, was slightly to the left. That building—Dr. Holbrook's lab—was completely dark. The barracks building had a few low lights burning, but it was pretty clear everyone was asleep.

Everyone except a lone guard who walked sentry duty. He turned the corner and walked out of sight, and the men on the beach advanced past Rose. They walked right past her. She wasn't there. They didn't see her.

Then, Jeff came up beside her. She looked up into his eyes and knew he could see her as she saw him. How, she had no idea, but somehow, they were present, together, in the vision, observing the same things and able to see each other. Freaky.

"We've got to stop this," she told him. "They're not the good guys, right?"

"Approaching at night in stealth gear?" He shook his head. "No. These are most definitely bad guys. But there aren't that many of them. We can handle this, now that we know about it. The thing is the timing. When is this? Any ideas for figuring that out?" he looked around him as if casting about for a clue.

But Rose knew what to do. "Look up. Note the stars. We can approximate based on weather, star position, phase of the moon. That sort of thing."

"Like regular ol' navigation, huh?" He looked up and took a good long look. "Where's my compass when I need it?"

"Back on whatever plane of existence our bodies are on," she told him. The clouds blew past, and the sky was exposed. "There's Sirius," she whispered.

"I've got a rough bearing. Since there's no moon that I can see, we can probably come up with a good guesstimate for date and time."

Just then, she heard the chime of the base clock and smiled. "We won't have to guess about the time, at least." She listened to the old clock in the distance with its muted bongs for the hour. Three and it stopped. "Three a.m."

"I'd like to see more of their approach," Jeff said. He made to walk forward, toward the barracks, but he couldn't move. "What?"

Rose knew what that meant. "There's more to see here. It won't let you go until you've seen what you need to. Look around. Notice everything. It could be something small."

She spun around to watch the waves, looking hard at the black ocean, but she didn't see anything.

Then, Jeff sucked in a breath. "See that?"

"What?"

"A periscope."

She caught a faint reflection of starlight on a tubular shape sticking up out of the water in the distance. Then, she was falling.

She shut her eyes against the disorientation, clinging to Jeff's hands as they fell out of the vision together and came back to the mostly bare room in Dr. Holbrook's lab building.

"A submarine?" she squawked, when she came back to herself. "Are you kidding me?"

Jeff shook his head and smiled in a resigned sort of way. "Sorry. Not kidding. The bad guys have a sub."

"That's bad." She couldn't even process how well funded the people after them must be in order to have a freaking submarine at their disposal. Were they backed by a rich government?

"Not as bad as it was when we didn't know about it," Jeff added. "Forewarned is forearmed."

She just shook her head at his grim optimism. "I hope you know what you're doing."

Jeff just smiled. "In a situation like this? Always."

"Who are these people? Why are they after us? And how in the world do they have access to a submarine?" She hadn't thought the enemy was so well equipped. The thought staggered her a bit. This was even more serious than she'd expected.

"State-funded from somewhere in the Middle East as far as we know. There are specialists trying to nail down exactly where the threat is coming from, but all we know for sure is that someone from that region is mad that we were given the gifts of the djinn, and they want them back. So far, it looks like they want to capture us—one at a time or in a group—and force us to use our powers for them." He shook his head. "If they really understood us, our training, and our gifts, they wouldn't even try. The old man with the turban chose us for a reason. We think it's because we're the good guys. Those who are looking to capture us are not, and that's why they didn't receive the gifts of their ancients."

"They want to make you work for them? That doesn't even make sense. How could they force you?" She shook her head, truly confused.

Jeff got quiet and looked at her with a very serious, slightly bashful expression. "If they captured you, or Casey, or some family member of one of the guys, they'd have really good leverage to force us into whatever they wanted."

That made her pause. Emotional blackmail. Yeah, she could see that. Hal would do anything and everything for Casey. That much was obvious. The idea that Jeff would do the same for herself had Rose's head spinning a bit.

"They came after me because they wanted to force you into working for them?" she asked, speaking her thoughts aloud without censoring them.

"Probably. They might have seen you as a way to get to me, or they might have wanted you for your own merits. They might think it would be best to fight fire with fire—our gifts against other people with gifts," he suggested. "We suspect there is at least a foreseer working on the wrong side because sometimes, they get a bit ahead of us in ways that could only happen if someone like you or I were feeding them information."

"It makes a warped kind of sense." Rose had to nod. "You said state-funded. So, this is like a government coming after us? How are we going to hold out against that?" Suddenly, she felt weak against the specter of such power.

"It's what we do for a living, Rosie," Jeff said, instilling some of his own confidence into her with his casual words. "I wouldn't have brought you here unless I knew we could protect you. Speaking of which…" He got up and headed for the door, then paused to look back when she didn't follow right away. "You coming? We've got to tell the guys about the invasion we just saw."

Rose shook her head and stood. She could see there would be no postponing the necessary meeting with the other guys. Jeff was full of energy and ready to take on the world, but she was less enthused about the danger that was heading their way. Still, she had to admit, he was the expert in that kind of situation. She had to follow his lead.

"Right behind you," she said, falling in behind the already-moving man headed back toward the barracks building next door.

The unit was already beginning to gather for the scheduled meeting when Jeff ushered Rosie into the room they used for planning their missions. The other guys went on alert as soon as they saw Jeff's face, and all casual discussion ended. Hal stood at the front of the room and gave them his attention.

"Captain, we've both foreseen an attack on this island," Jeff reported without preamble. He had everyone's attention now.

"When and where?" Hal was just as to the point.

"They come out of the water on the beach where we do PT. As for when... Just before oh-three-hundred on a moonless night with scattered cloud cover," Jeff fired back.

Over the next twenty minutes, the team asked questions, and Rosie and Jeff answered them as best they could. Jeff was astounded to learn the minute details Rosie had observed and her ability to recall them. They took turns going through the exact sequence of what they'd seen, and her account seemed to have a lot more nuance and fine detail than his. He supposed it was her years of doing this that made her so much better at it than him, but if he'd needed any convincing that she knew her stuff, he had it. From the impressed looks of the other guys, they saw it, too.

"New moon is tonight," Hal said when they settled in to discuss the details of what they'd seen.

"It felt imminent," Rosie contributed. "Some visions have a feeling of urgency about them that means they're going to happen sooner rather than later. This was one of those."

"And you both were in the same vision?" Hal asked. "How does that work?"

"That was a new one," Rosie admitted. "I've never shared a vision with anyone before, but we were both definitely there in the same moment. We were able to see each other and talk inside the vision."

Hal gave them both a strange look but nodded. "Well, what we need is a plan," he said finally, rubbing his hands together.

Hal started issuing orders, and within moments, the room had been transformed into a war room. One of the guys brought up a map of the island and used the room's projector to display it against the wall. Hal had them walk through the details again, and zeroed in on the section of beach they'd been on in the vision.

"There's just one more thing," Jeff added as they went through the sequence again. The first time they'd done it, there had been so many questions about the details, he'd never gotten to the final moments of the display.

Hal looked at him expectantly. "What is it?"

"Just before the vision ended, I saw a periscope out on the water," he admitted.

Hal sat back as he whistled between his teeth. "Frogmen and a sub?" he mused. "This just got a whole lot more interesting."

They broke for lunch about two hours later, all adjourning to the mess hall for some refreshment. When they went back to planning, Rosie opted to go back to the lab building to talk over the dual-vision phenomenon with Dr. Holbrook. Jeff knew the planning session would be going on for hours yet, and if there were any details they needed Rosie for, he could just pop over and ask her.

He insisted on walking her over to the other building before rejoining the unit in the war room. Nobody objected, and when he returned to the planning session, more than one guy commented about how good Rosie's recall had been. It seemed she had unanimously impressed them all. Jeff felt an unaccustomed pride fill him. She really was something special.

He spent the rest of the day closeted with the guys, planning for the action that might come as early as that very night. All other routine work was postponed, without making it obvious from the outside that they were up to something unique—just in case they were being watched from the sea. Which they probably were.

Hal operated mostly autonomously from base command, which was a good thing in this case. There was an admiral to whom he now reported in the Spec Ops command, but a simple phone call to the man—Admiral Morrow—had given Hal carte blanche to handle any perceived threat against Plum Island. The admiral had called the base commander and given him the same orders, reinforcing the idea that Hal's group had specialized skills, and the projects housed on that island were all of vital interest to the military.

Phrased in that way, the commander in charge of the island—a fellow named Kinkaid—had become very cooperative in allowing Hal to run the show as far as the defense of the island went. Although there were

MPs and a few combat-experienced troopers on the island, there wasn't really any expectation of trouble on base. The few workers here were mostly on long-term research projects that didn't require the kind of rapid response that other locations used. After all, they were on an isolated island in friendly waters. As long as they controlled who came and went from the base, that had always been enough.

Until now.

Luckily, Hal's group was used to dealing with unusual and hostile situations. They were the reason a sub was even now trolling the waters just off the coast, and they were the ones the bad guys were after. It was only fitting that Hal and his men be the ones to deal with the threat. They had the usual armament they brought into the field and had received permission to utilize any of the base's equipment they might require.

Given that leeway, the men were able to devise a plan that might just make the opposition think twice about ever attacking this island again.

CHAPTER EIGHT

Rose spent her afternoon discussing the shared-vision phenomenon with Dr. Holbrook and catching up with the woman she hadn't seen in years. When Rose tried to ask questions about Jeff's abilities and Jeana's opinions about what they'd discovered so far, she hit a brick wall. Jeana explained that she didn't want Rose to get any preconceptions about what might or might not work with Jeff. She wanted Rose's approach to be fresh and intuitive, not influenced by anything that might have happened in the recent past.

Rose understood, but she was still very curious about what Jeff had been able to do and learn on his own and with Jeana's help. He had a tactical mind and had noticed things Rose hadn't in that shared vision, but she'd been at this longer, and when they'd done the report to Hal and the other guys, Rose had felt glad she'd been able to prove she had a place among this group. That she could bring some skills to the table.

She had no doubt Jeff would pick up fast on the things she could teach him, but at least for the moment, she felt like she could really contribute to his progress. What would happen when she'd taught him all she knew? Well, she'd cross that bridge when they got to it. If they wanted to boot her off the island and away from the safety it represented, then she'd just have to figure something else out.

For now, they had to foil the attack that she felt sure would come either tonight or tomorrow. Hal had told Rose to fill Jeana in on the vision and help the doc prepare her lab for possible intrusion. Once Jeana heard the details, she pulled out a sheaf of papers in a red folder that had been in her desk. It was a plan for removing sensitive data from the lab area for just this kind of situation.

"You can always trust the military to have a procedure in place for every contingency," Jeana said with a grim smile as she handed over a copy of the procedure to Rose. "I'd appreciate whatever help you can give me on this. We don't have a lot of personnel here, right now. Once the powers that be decided this wasn't some sort of medical problem, they shipped the infectious disease folks back to their regular duty stations. I was brought in and advised to choose members for my team very carefully. They really don't want details about these guys to spread, and I don't blame them."

"I'm happy to help," Rose replied easily as she leafed through the three-page procedure. "It looks like mostly we're just removing hard drives and leaving the empty shells of the computers like decoys or something."

"Exactly," Jeana replied with a grin. She went to the closet in her office and withdrew a briefcase. Placing it on the desk, she opened it up to show Rose. "This was made specifically for my work computers. The foam is cut for every piece and includes a little foam envelope for my laptop. The case itself is armored shielded, and once locked, if tampered with, it will destroy the magnetic media inside. So, even if the bad guys get the case, it's highly unlikely they could get to the data."

"Wow." Rose was impressed.

"This won't take too long, but I could use a hand with the desktop units. There are two, and we can do them simultaneously if you'll follow my lead." Jeana turned to offer Rose a small screwdriver, which she took.

"Just tell me what to do."

By dinnertime, they were as ready as they could be. All the sensitive data from Jeana's lab was in the base vault, in its armed briefcase that would self-destruct if anyone messed with it. Jeana, herself, was staying at the base commander's house, ostensibly a dinner guest of the commander's wife. The plan was for the dinner to run long and Jeana would be invited to sleep over in their guest room. That would keep her on the other side of the island and, hopefully, out of harm's way.

Hal had wanted to tuck Rose away in the same fashion, but she'd argued against it. If she got hit with a vision during the attack, she wanted to be on the spot where she could tell the guys. Likewise, if Jeff got the vision, she wanted to be there to help him interpret it. She didn't know why she was so adamant about wanting to be there, but she felt the need to stake out her territory, and that was in the barracks, near the action.

"You know, you really don't have to stay. I managed this far without your insight into my visions," Jeff argued. "I can handle this."

"I'm sure you can, and my desire to stay isn't intended as an insult to your abilities," she tried to explain. "I just... I need to be here. I don't know why, yet, but I do know that I need to be close."

Jeff looked into her eyes, as if searching for the answers within, then seemed to give up and shook his head. "I don't like it, but I respect your position."

They went into the mess hall together and sat with Hal and Casey to share the meal. Casey had also rejected the idea of being stashed somewhere safe while the men dealt with the threat, and Hal had relented. Casey and Rose would stick together, out of the way but still in the barracks building.

They'd agreed to meet by the big ladies' room and hold tight there until given the all clear. The bad guys would be looking for offices and fortified safe rooms if they made it into the building. It was reasonable to assume that the ladies' room would be low on their list of target areas, so it seemed the safest place to be if they were going to stay.

After dinner ended, Jeff insisted on taking Rose on a tour of the ladies' room. It seemed an odd thing, but she went along with him. Jeff walked in confidently, heading for the row of shower stalls. He reached into one of them, yanking hard on the shower head, which caused an audible click. Then, he reached over to the tall linen cabinet beside that shower stall and pressed inward until it popped back, as if on a spring. The whole cabinet pivoted on hidden hinges and revealed a hidden chamber.

"When we did the remodeling, we put in a hidden room behind the showers," Jeff explained. "It's not huge, but it'll fit you and Casey easily, with room to spare. There's even a cot, two chairs, and some communications gear." He gestured for her to follow him inside the hidden compartment. "You have feeds from the hidden closed-circuit cameras we rigged around the building and in some of the corridors." He flipped a switch on a large screen hung on one wall, and it came to life. It showed several camera views, separated into boxes on the screen. "In particular, there's a camera positioned to view the hallway and the door to the ladies' room. From here, you can see if the coast is clear outside. Or, if anyone enters the ladies' room from the hallway, you can see just who it is."

"That's pretty amazing," Rose allowed. "Does Casey know about this?"

"Sure. She was here when we built it," he replied easily, turning off the monitor. "You two should stay in here throughout. If you need to get in touch with any of us, use the radios, but do it sparingly. We need to concentrate on the mission."

"Understood." She looked at the radios on the small table next to the cot. They were sitting in charging stations, and there were two of them.

"Casey is trained to report anything she might see on the cameras to Hal. We practiced with her until she had our lingo down pat," he told Rose as they exited the safe room. "She's familiar with the radios and the frequencies we use. Follow her lead for now. Once this is over, we'll see about getting you up to speed on our procedures. If you're staying with us, you need a bit of practice outside of real-world situations." He smiled at her, and she knew he was trying to ease the tension that had crept up on her.

It was hitting home that this was going to be dangerous. Not just for her. She'd be safely ensconced in a hidden room. But Jeff—and all the guys—would be out there, fighting the bad guys. What if something happened to him? She'd be devastated if he got hurt...or worse.

"Hey," he said, putting his knuckle under her chin to raise her head gently so their eyes could meet. "It's going to be okay."

"Sorry. It just became a little too real all of a sudden," she admitted.

Jeff tugged her gently into his arms, right there next to the showers. Being in his arms felt so good. So safe. So warm and protected. She hugged him back, reveling in the feeling she had never felt before in her adult life. This was special. This man was special.

She turned her head into his neck and kissed him there, wanting him to know how much she appreciated him and his embrace. She hadn't quite anticipated the fire that started to flow in her veins at the touch of her lips against his skin, but she supposed she should have realized what would happen. They were simply combustible when they got together. She'd learned that lesson very well, indeed, last night.

"Oh, Rosie," Jeff groaned, pulling away only slightly so that he could look down into her eyes. "You're killing me."

She smiled, knowing his words weren't a complaint. "You have the same effect on me," she admitted, hearing the breathiness of her own voice.

Jeff looked around the room, as if considering their options, then bent slightly to grip her under each thigh with his large, strong, capable hands. He carried her as if she weighed nothing at all, moving directly into the shower stall at the end of the row, farthest from the door.

Luckily, they were somewhat roomy shower stalls. Each had its curtained alcove, though they were all in a row. He pulled the curtain shut behind them and then set her on her feet, her back brushing the tiled wall behind her. The shower stall might be roomy for one, but it was deliciously crowded with both of them in there. She couldn't wait to find out what he had in mind.

"I don't have a lot of time," he told her, almost apologetically.

"I don't mind," she whispered back, knowing whatever happened next, she wanted this time alone with him. She wanted him. Period.

"Are you sure?" He cupped her cheek with one hand, looking deep into her eyes. "It'll have to be fast."

"Then, let's not waste any more time," she told him, already tugging his shirt from his waistband.

She saw the grin on his face as he took over the task and took the shirt off over his head. She did the same, leaving only her bra, which had dried overnight, along with her panties. She lowered the borrowed sweatpants but left the panties. It was his turn to get rid of his pants.

But he had boots on, and those pants weren't going to come off all the way. He lowered them a bit, but left the crucial bit covered for now, while he returned to her, stroking her skin with his calloused, skilled hands.

As his head lowered and his lips touched hers, she felt her bra straps slide down her shoulders. Then, he was kissing her, and she lost track a bit of what was happening. The cool air of the room against her nipples alerted her when he peeled the lacy cups of her bra away from her breasts. A second later, his warm hands took away the momentary chill and started shivers of an altogether different kind coursing down her spine.

He broke off the kiss and trailed his lips down her neck and over the mounds of her breasts before latching onto an erect nipple. Meanwhile, his hands went to the scrap of lace and elastic at her hips, lowering it until it slipped down her legs to pool on the shower floor. She stepped out of the panties and lifted one knee so she could get closer to him.

At that point, he lowered his pants enough to free himself, allowing her wet core to slide up against the thick erection that she wanted so badly. He felt so good. Tall and strong and hard where she was soft. She felt like they belonged together, odd as that seemed after such a short acquaintance.

"Don't make me wait," she begged him, wanting him to know she was ready and willing.

He groaned. "You definitely are killing me, sweetheart. Killing me so good."

He lifted her by the hips, and they fit together just right. On the downward slide, he pushed inside her, and she took him gratefully.

Yes. That's exactly what she wanted. To be possessed. Filled. Complete.

Then, he began to move. Sweet mother in heaven, that felt so damned great.

It was hard. It was fast. It was real and good. He stole her breath with his staccato movements. Then, he gave it back again, along with a pleasure the likes of which she could easily get addicted to. God help her, she was going to miss him if and when they parted.

But she couldn't think about that now.

She held on for dear life as he pounded into her, pressing her back against the shower wall. The fabric curtain at his back moved with his efforts, making a sliding noise that made her want to chuckle, but the way he moved inside her was no laughing matter. It was all serious. All consuming.

She came hard, and he followed a moment later, biting back a groan. She was fairly confident that nobody had come into the ladies' room while they'd been frolicking in the shower stall, but she couldn't be absolutely sure. She hadn't really been paying attention to much of anything except Jeff there for a good long while.

But who could blame her?

"That was amazing," she whispered to him as they came down together from a momentous height.

He kissed the top of her head in a gentle gesture that touched her heart. "You are amazing, Rosie. You rock my world, over and over."

"Back at you, Jeeves." She was feeling a bit naughty after making love with him in a somewhat public place where they could've been discovered at any time. Mischief lit her soul.

"I think that's the first time you've ever used

my call sign," he replied. "I like it. I may never hear it the same way again."

She pushed at his shoulder in a playful way. "Just for that, Jeffrey, I think you should do what we just did, again. Later. When we have more time."

"With the greatest pleasure, milady, I assure you. Once things are settled, you're going to have to kick me out of your bed to get me to leave."

"I'll hold you to that, mister. Just see if I don't."

After Jeff left, Rose took a shower, cleaning up all evidence of their activities. She dressed in a spare set of sweats from the linen cabinet and prepared herself for the night ahead as best she could. There wasn't much time left before she was supposed to meet Casey, so she just stayed in the ladies' room, practicing the trick of opening the secret room and switching on the monitor and radios.

She was watching the camera displays, seeing the men preparing for their evening watch. Not that there was much to see. They went about their business as if everything was normal when on screen, but she knew there were places not covered by the cameras where they were preparing for the night's dangerous work.

They weren't taking any chances. The cameras might've been put up by them and run in a closed circuit, but they weren't counting on their surveillance staying private. There weren't any wireless signals that could be hacked, but even in a wired system, there were ways in for skilled operatives.

Jeff had told her that they'd weighed the options and decided to risk the camera installations, only after very careful consideration of each and every angle. What resulted was a system that the men knew inside and out. They knew the exact boundaries of what the cameras covered…and, more importantly, what they did not.

The tactical radios would remain silent until operations began. Even then, the men would be speaking in their own code, and only when absolutely necessary. Still, Rose switched on the radio, just in case. She longed to hear Jeff's voice.

Something had changed between them. Their quickie in the shower stall had been laced with desperation, but also with…love? That's what she felt, deep in her heart, and that's what she believed she perceived coming from Jeff, as well.

She couldn't really say why she was so sure. Maybe it was just wishful thinking. Or, maybe, it was some heretofore unknown byproduct of her gift. Somehow, she sensed that he was growing to love her. Still, he hadn't said the words. Not even close.

She would do her best not to pressure him. She wouldn't say it first. For one thing, she wasn't really sure whether or not she could trust this weird gut feeling. For another, she wasn't sure what declaring themselves would mean for them.

Could they have a relationship when everything was so up in the air? Casey and Hal seemed to make things work, but Casey had mentioned that she'd known Hal most of her life since he was her big brother's best friend. They had a long history. They had known each other long before anything had happened to change Hal into what he had become.

Rose didn't have any history with Jeff. At times, that didn't seem to matter at all. They shared a gift of foreknowledge. Jeff knew more about the challenges that kind of gift brought than any man she had ever known. That forged a bond. A quick, hard bond that meant a lot to her even after such a short time.

In her saner moments, she thought she must be deluding herself. She was probably letting a healthy dose of lust, and a crazy situation, get to her. She was imagining things. Wanting to believe there was more between them than just hormones and coincidental timing.

Rose was trying the mechanism for the hidden door again, when Casey came into the room. She had a small cooler in one hand and a shopping bag in the other.

"I brought snacks," she said with false bravado. "I see Jeeves showed you around the special accommodations." She nodded toward the secret door Rose had just opened again. "Let's get settled in, shall we? Hal said, if anything's going to happen tonight, it'll start soon. He wants us buttoned up."

CHAPTER NINE

Rose went inside the hidden room, and Casey followed suit. After taking one last look around the ladies' room to make sure they hadn't left anything to indicate where they were going, they closed the hidden door and locked themselves in. Rose knew they were locked away for the duration now, and it made her feel just a little claustrophobic.

Casey turned the monitor back on and that helped. Being able to see what was going on around the building helped a lot. Especially when Rose caught sight of Jeff walking slowly into camera range and pausing there, looking at something in his hands.

Closer inspection revealed he had a cell phone in his hands, and he was playing some sort of game. Rose had never seen him do anything of the sort, and she realized he was lingering in the camera's view on purpose. For her.

"That's really sweet," Casey commented. "He probably knows you're worried."

"How do you know he's doing it on purpose?" Rose asked, curious about Casey's thoughts on the matter.

"Jeeves doesn't play games on his phone. None of the guys do. At least, not that I've seen. And they all know where the cameras are. If he's visible, it's with intent. This is probably part of their plan in case the bad guys somehow got into their camera feed—which Hal says is next to impossible, but they aren't leaving anything to chance. So, if somebody is watching, they see a guy not on alert. Playing video games. Bored. If nobody but us is watching, we see Jeeves hanging out, safe. It helps both ways."

"Sneaky," Rose mused. "But I appreciate the thought that went into it. I admit, it's good to see him. This whole situation has me on edge."

"Me too," Casey admitted. "Which is why I brought hot cocoa. I can't do alcohol because of the baby, but chocolate is always good to cure what ails you. Am I right?" Casey grinned.

"I can't argue with that logic," Rose said in reply. "Good thinking." Casey dug out two mugs from the shopping bag and began pouring out steaming hot cocoa from a big thermos.

Rose felt a little better after sipping the cocoa, but she still watched the clock.

According to what she and Jeff had seen in their vision, the action could start any time now. Jeff had long since put away his phone and stepped out of camera range. He and his friends were no doubt in hiding in readiness for whatever might happen next.

It could be that they had the day wrong, and the attack would come tomorrow night. In that case, tonight would have been a dress rehearsal for the real thing. But, as the night deepened, Rose got a creepy feeling between her shoulders that something was about to happen. Something big.

Maybe it was just nerves. Casey had been upbeat at first. She'd been a good companion and had brought a huge picnic of treats to keep them amused, but Rose knew Casey had to be worrying about Hal.

"Three a.m., right?" Casey said in a subdued tone, her voice barely carrying to where Rose sat, staring at the monitor.

Rose turned to her. "That's our best estimate," she confirmed.

"We're almost there now." Casey's tone was contemplative, tinged with fear.

"We might have the night wrong," Rose allowed.

"But you don't think so."

"How did you know?" Rose heard the surprise in her own voice.

"I may not be a mutant, but I'm pretty good with people. Your shoulders are very tight, and you look worried," Casey explained.

Rose deliberately rolled her shoulders to try

to ease the tension. "I'm not a mutant."

Casey looked startled then laughed, as Rose had intended, when she saw the teasing smile on Rose's face.

"Sorry. It's just hard sometimes, being the only one here without superpowers," Casey admitted. Rose was about to reply when a flicker of motion on one of the camera feeds caught her eye.

"Holy crap. It's happening!" she scream-whispered. Casey jumped up from her seated position on the cot and came over to crowd alongside Rose in front of the big monitor screen.

"Where?"

Rose pointed to one of the boxes the screen was divided into. This camera angle looked out from the back of the building toward the water. The camera must've been placed near the roof of the building because it showed a good portion of the yard behind the building and even a bit of the beach. The infrared sensors picked up everything in shades of gray.

"See that?" Rose put her finger on a black shape on the screen that nearly blended into the other black shapes...but not enough. "It's a guy in a wet suit."

Casey squinted. "How do you...? Oh." The man turned his head and the little round face hole in the headgear showed a man's profile. "Damn. I'd hoped you were wrong."

"Me too."

Jeff felt the change in the air the moment

the first of the enemy soldiers began crawling up out of the ocean. Hot damn. They'd been right. He hadn't really doubted the vision, but it was still a marvel to him when something he foresaw came to pass.

The team had been positioned strategically all around the expected infiltration zone. He and Rose had sketched out the positions of the enemy they'd seen in their shared vision, but the unit hadn't taken anything for granted in planning this mission. They'd prepared for everything Jeff had seen—and more. Hal had asked for, and received, backup from the base command. The commander had called on the Navy for any assets they had in the area.

Hal hadn't shared what, exactly, the Navy was going to do about the submarine off the coast of Long Island, but he'd looked pleased when he came back from his last meeting with the commander earlier. Jeff didn't want to speculate, but he and the rest of the guys took Hal at his word when he said the submarine would be dealt with one way or another.

Their job was to protect the beach and not let any of the enemy troops infiltrate the island. A click over the earpieces that all the members of the unit wore told them the game was afoot. Their carefully laid plans were in motion, but they all knew that pre-made plans only lasted for a short time once things started really happening. They would adapt and overcome...as always.

Jeff spared a thought for Rosie. Sweet, sweet Rosie. She was literally the girl of his dreams, and when this was over, he was going to tell her how he felt—short acquaintance or not. He felt something special—make that really special—when they were together. It wasn't just the sex, though that was phenomenal. It was a feeling of belonging. Of fitting together like two halves of a whole.

He'd never felt like this before, and he suspected he never would again, about any woman. Jeff figured he was in love with Rosie, though heaven knew they'd only known each other a short time. Maybe that was all it took? Maybe you didn't have to know someone most of your life like Hal and Casey. Maybe all it took was finding the right person at the right time and trusting the instincts that told Jeff that he would be forever incomplete if he let Rosie go.

Yeah, maybe that was it. Or, maybe he was crazy. He wasn't entirely sure, but he'd give it a go as soon as he got her alone again. He wanted to find out if he was alone in these wild, unexpected feelings or if, maybe, she was feeling something similar. He knew things would be a whole lot easier on his nerves if he knew for sure she felt the same way.

Decision made, with a resolute heart, he went into battle. The enemy wouldn't stand a chance. Nothing that stood between him and Rosie would ever defeat him. No how. No way.

Jeff walked through the enemy like he was plowing a field. They fell, left and right of him, dark shapes in the pitch black of the sandy dunes. He was wearing night vision gear, as was the whole unit. The bad guys had their own version, which looked like a foreign make. Maybe something out of Europe or the old Soviet Union. They'd have to examine the enemy gear later.

For now, Jeff was using all his skill and stealth to dart the enemy with super-fast-acting knockout drugs. They were trying not to kill anyone if they didn't have to. They wanted prisoners to interrogate so they could learn more about where this attack had come from and just who these people were.

That's why the front line had been issued air guns with highly effective darts. They were nearly silent with the background of waves lapping at the shoreline and the other night sounds, so it was easy to drop quite a few of the enemy at some distance with just a couple of sharpshooters using dart rifles. Jeff's group was doing cleanup closer in, with handguns. He trusted what he'd seen in the vision to tell him where the enemy was hiding, though after a few moments, the future had changed, and the vision was unreliable.

Their action had altered what he'd foreseen. Hopefully, they'd changed it for the better, but only time would tell.

Rose was watching the monitor in the hidden room when her vision clouded, and a premonition hit her. She grabbed onto the table to keep steady in the real world while she closed her eyes and let her gift take her away to a future possibility.

She was in the ladies' room. Not the hidden room where she was in reality, but the outer room where the facilities were located. She was standing off to one side, observing as a strange man, dressed all in black, paced around the room like a caged lion. This couldn't be good.

"When is this?" Jeff's voice came to her from behind. She spun, and there he was, on the vision-plane with her.

"Are you really here or are you part of the vision?" she asked, just to be sure.

"We're sharing it again, apparently," he confirmed. "Is this happening now? Is it soon or is it later? Tomorrow? Days from now?"

"Hard to tell without obvious markers. There's nothing with a date on it in here." She looked all around as the man in their vision did the same. He was searching for something. She was searching for clues about when this might take place in reality.

"That blue towel was there when I left earlier," Jeff offered, pointing toward a discarded towel in one corner of the room that Rose knew she hadn't tidied. Her blood ran cold.

"I left it there. This is tonight," she whispered, fear clutching at her heart. "Is he looking for me and Casey?"

The man in the vision kept moving, oblivious to his watchers, and sniffed loudly as he zeroed in on the shower pipe that hid the opening mechanism to the hidden door. Something about his actions raised a flag in Rose's mind. She'd seen something like this before.

"I'd say that's a roger," Jeff said in a grim voice. "I'm back on the beach. How long do I have to get to you once this vision clears?" he asked in clipped tones.

Rose's mind spun for a moment. There had to be a way to figure this out. There just had to be!

"Wait a sec. I'm going to try something." Rose used all her hard-won skills to try to divide her attention away from the vision and back to the real world where she sat, clutching the small table, crowded in next to Casey. She made herself speak aloud, hoping Casey would realize what was going on, but kept her eyes firmly shut, so as to avoid too much disorientation. "Casey?"

"Rose? Are you okay?"

"Vision," she said shortly. "Man in outer room. What do you see on cameras?"

"Holy shit!" she heard Casey mutter as she tapped some keys and brought up larger images of the inside of the building. "Okay. I see... Wait a minute... Nothing in the hallway just outside the ladies' room, but there's a door open in the mess hall. I don't think any of our guys would've left a door open."

Rose related what Casey had said to Jeff, and he swore as the man in the vision successfully opened the secret door. "Tell Casey to call it in. Use the radio. They already suspect you two are here, anyway. The moment I get out of this vision, I'm on my way to you, Rose." He reached for her, and the moment he touched her in the vision, it disintegrated.

Well, that was one way to end the vision state. She'd have to remember that, if they ever ended up in the same vision again. The way things were going with them, it seemed like the possibility was more probable than not.

Jeff came back from the vision to find himself alone on the beach, well hidden behind a sand dune, thank goodness. Casey's voice, speaking in the code they'd taught her, came over the headset just a split second after he started running for the building.

His unit had his back. They'd neutralized the enemy on the beach and gave Jeff a clear run for the open door to the mess hall. No doubt, that was the route the man in black had used to get into the building. Jeff would be right behind him.

Jeff heard Casey's report over the radio when the enemy soldier entered camera range in the hallway outside the ladies' room. Jeff ran faster, even as he tried not to alert the bastard to his presence.

"He's at the door," Casey reported, and Jeff could hear the terror in her voice over the radio. Damn. "He's opening the door to the ladies' room. He's going inside. We can't see him, but he's inside," Casey's voice dropped to a whisper. "Rose says he'll be searching around for a minute or two before he finds the hidden door mechanism. I'm going quiet now, just in case."

Jeff was at the door to the hallway. He

opened it as quietly as he could then made his way rapidly down the hall to the door to the ladies' room. He'd seen what the soldier was doing. He had a moment to prepare himself for the confrontation. After checking his weapons, he crashed through the door. Surprise would be his greatest asset in this fight.

"I know I objected to the idea of a camera in the ladies' room, but Hal was right. We need some way to see what's just outside this hidden door if we ever have to hide in here again," Casey whispered to Rose. She was tense with nerves, but Casey was holding together remarkably well. "This door is locked, but it's not the heavy security door Hal wants to install. He had to have that specially made and it's not ready yet. This one is good, but if that guy out there finds it, he might be able to get in if he tries hard enough. It'll take time, though."

"He's going to find it. I saw that much," Rose told Casey.

"Shit," Casey swore.

"But Jeff is coming. He saw it too. He knows what's happening." Rose tried to inject some confidence into her whispered words, but sensed she'd failed by Casey's tense expression.

Rose knew what the man outside was doing. They still had a few minutes before he'd find the hidden door. Determined to defend them, should it be necessary, Rose opened every cupboard in the room and looked for something they could use, just in case Jeff ran late. The first slim cabinets held blankets and canned food, but on her third try, she struck pay dirt.

There were sticks—fighting sticks like martial artists used. There was also a handgun in a case. Casey slapped her forehead with one palm in the universal gesture of someone who's forgotten something important.

"Hal taught me how to use this," she whispered, taking the handgun from Rose and expertly checking the ammunition. "Do you mind?"

"Better you have it, since you know how," Rose whispered back.

She took the longer of the two fighting sticks and positioned herself to one side of the hidden door. If the man she'd seen opened it before help could arrive, he would get a surprise. She would trip the guy up with the stick, if possible, and hopefully, Casey could shoot him.

All this time, Rose had been counting down in her mind the actions she'd seen the man take in the vision. If nothing changed, he should be finding the door mechanism in another twenty to thirty seconds. After that, it was just a matter of how long it took him to break in.

"Get ready. If he's coming in, it'll be soon," Rose told Casey in the lowest tone she could manage. She held up one hand, counting down the time in her head. She listened hard for the snick of the door, but after thirty seconds, it hadn't come, and she realized the future she'd seen in the vision had changed. "I don't hear anything. Jeff must have stopped him," she said, trying to hold the worry in check as much as she could.

Casey's hands were steady, but her eyes were wide with nerves. "Thank heavens."

"Don't let your guard down. The future we saw changed, but I don't know what it's become. They could be fighting for their lives on the other side of this door, right now."

"When this is all over, we're putting in a peephole or something."

Jeff crashed through the door from the hallway just as the intruder zeroed in on the shower head that would lead to the secret door. The man spun around, without triggering the hidden door, and launched himself at Jeff.

Jeff's darts went wild and missed the man who moved more fluidly than anyone Jeff had ever seen. But he didn't care. This guy was going down. Hard. He'd dared to go after the women—to go after Rose—and that could not be allowed to go unpunished.

The enemy spun a roundhouse kick out of nowhere, sending the dart gun flying across the room and numbing Jeff's thumb and wrist. Hell, it could be broken, but he couldn't think about it now. Not when he was closing in for a hand-to-hand contest with this big fucker who moved like a shadow.

Jeff let fly with the martial arts skills he'd perfected even before he'd joined the military. In the years since becoming a professional soldier, he'd only improved his form, and he'd learned every dirty street fighting trick in the

FUTURE PAST

book, as well. He pulled out all the stops as the fight engaged, moving faster than thought, faster than reflexes. This was pure adrenaline and instinct. Deadly dangerous instinct.

Hands and feet flew in a flurry of motion. Jeff was pushed to his limits when a flash of insight told him to zig when the enemy zagged, putting him in the perfect position. The soldier went down with an audible crunch, hitting his head hard on the tile floor. Damn. Jeff didn't want to kill the guy. He just wanted to take the man out of the action, not crack his skull in the middle of the ladies' room. For one thing, Casey would never forgive him for christening her décor in such a way.

He approached cautiously, making sure the enemy was down for the count before relaxing his guard even the tiniest bit. There was blood on the floor under the man's head, and he didn't move a muscle as Jeff first prodded him with a boot toe, then got close enough to disarm him. Only then, did Jeff make contact with his teammates over the radio.

Hal pushed through the ladies' room door even before Jeff was finished checking in. Two more of the guys were right behind him. Hal took stock of the situation and began issuing orders.

"Zeke. Dan. Take the prisoner out of here. Put him on a table in the mess hall and have Rick take a look," Hal said, moving around to block the hidden door should the prisoner somehow pop up and start fighting again.

Neither Hal nor Jeff relaxed until the others

had left with the fallen man. Then, they sprung into action. Hal went over to the shower head to pop the door while Jeff went to stand to one side of the cabinet that masked the hidden entrance.

"We're secure," Jeff heard Hal tell Casey over the radio. "Coming in."

CHAPTER TEN

Rose sagged in relief when the cabinet swung open and Jeff and Hal were on the other side. She put the long stick she'd been holding to one side and watched with relief as Casey threw herself into Hal's arms. Hal intercepted the handgun, still in Casey's hand, and kept it safe while his woman burst into tears of sheer joy and relief.

Rose felt the same, but she couldn't be quite as demonstrative. Knowing the future had led her to learn control over showing too much of her emotions from a young age. She met Jeff's gaze, and she felt tears gather in her eyes. Tears of relief that she refused to let fall, but she felt them, nonetheless. Jeff nodded. He understood. She could read it in his expression.

Hal ushered Casey out of the small room,

and Rose followed, noting the bloodstain on the floor. Jeff touched her arm, and she turned to him.

"You fought him?" she asked. She had seen the man in her vision. He'd been a big brute. The idea that Jeff had gone up against him made a shiver race down her spine. Whether of fear or admiration, she wasn't exactly sure.

"He went down harder than I wanted, but the guys are working on him now. We wanted at least one to question and maybe send back to carry the message," he said in a low voice as they followed Hal and Casey out of the large ladies' room.

"What message?" Rose wanted to know.

"The message that intruders onto this island will be dealt with accordingly," Hal said over his shoulder.

"We're putting all the guys we knocked out into a raft and setting it adrift," Jeff elaborated. "We'll keep an eye on them from above with a high-flying drone, but basically, we want their people to pick them up, take them away, and never try a stunt like this again."

"Why not take prisoners?" Rose wanted to know.

Hal cringed, shaking his head. "Too complicated. We're on U.S. soil. If we take a bunch of prisoners, there would be a lot of explaining to do. A paper trail. Possibly an international incident. We can get away with questioning the one guy because we can do that quietly, among ourselves and a trusted few who regularly deal with top secret ops. But if we start filling up a prison somewhere with these guys, questions are going to be asked."

Rose thought about it and realized he was right. "Are you sure you got them all?" She hadn't really thought they would be able to knock out the men she'd seen in her vision with dart guns, but the guys had been adamant in not wanting to kill anybody on U.S. soil. Rose suspected there were legalities involved that she didn't fully understand.

"Every last one but the guy who made it into the ladies' room. I still don't understand how he got past us," Jeff admitted, sounding very concerned about that little lapse.

As well he should. But there was something she'd noticed in the quick vision of the man in the ladies' room. Something she'd seen before and didn't really understand, but knew just enough to say that it was unusual.

"Did you notice the way the guy was sniffing?" Rose asked Jeff as they walked past the mess hall.

She vaguely noted that most of the men were in there, clustered around one of the far tables, where a light was shining brightly down over someone who lay on the table. Jeff and Hal didn't stop, however, heading farther down the main hall to the common room of the building that acted like a big living room for the unit.

"Yeah, that seemed odd," Jeff replied, following Hal and Casey into the common room. Hal ushered Casey to one of the big couches along the far wall, but Jeff and Rose paused just inside the doors, giving the other couple an illusion of privacy for the moment.

"I've seen that before," she told him. "I'm not sure what it means, but whenever I see someone do that in a vision, that person proves to have special skills when and if I actually see them."

"Skills? Like what?"

Jeff was all business now, and Rose appreciated it. She might want to crawl into his arms the way Casey was doing with Hal, but not in public. She wasn't used to displaying her emotions as freely as the other couple. Perhaps she never would be. She was glad Jeff was giving her a bit of space. Maybe later...in private...she would be able to fall apart a bit, but right now, there was still information to pass along. Sometimes, it felt like the message was the most important thing. The most imperative thing in the universe. This was one of those times.

"One time, I was sitting in a coffee shop with a good view of the street outside, and I foresaw a purse snatching that I didn't have time to stop. The woman was preoccupied, bending low and sniffing around like that guy, earlier. She was looking for something, I thought. A criminal used her distraction to make a grab for her purse, only she was stronger than she looked, and she held onto the bag, using it to spin the jerk around and into a nearby tree." She cringed at the memory of the way the assailant's arm had bled after breaking against the hard bark. "He didn't get her purse, but he did get arrested after being sent to the hospital. While he lay bleeding and unconscious by the tree, the woman went back to her sniffing as if what she'd done was nothing at all. A minute later, she smiled as she retrieved a hat from where it was stuck, and very well hidden, behind a mailbox. She brushed the hat off, rolled it up and stuck it in her bag before walking off without a second glance at the guy who'd tried to mug her. She was gone before the cops showed up. Someone in the coffee shop had called them after noticing the guy bleeding out the window."

"Was she some kind of Mata Hari?" Jeff mused. "I've not met many, but there are some female operatives in the intelligence world who are reputed to have those kinds of skills."

"She didn't look like a spy. Just a woman searching for her hat," Rose insisted. "Another time, there was a guy doing that sniffing thing. There wasn't a vision involved. I actually just saw him back behind the store when I went out to dump the trash in the big bin. He stopped as soon as he saw me and took off running. I've never seen any human being run that fast, and I've never seen anybody hurdle an eight-foot fence in one leaping bound. What he did looked humanly impossible. There were others just like that, over the years, too."

"So, you're saying the sniffing guy from tonight might be more than he looks?" Jeff asked, his brows drawing together in concern.

She nodded. "You should warn whoever is watching him. If he has physical skills like those others I've seen in visions and in real life, then he could surprise you."

Jeff put one hand on her shoulder and looked deep into her eyes. "Are you okay if I leave you here for a moment?"

"Yes." She nodded again, swallowing hard against the emotion that demanded she hug him tight and never let go. She couldn't do that. Not yet. Not while there was still work to do and messages to deliver. "Go tell them."

Jeff didn't come back to the common room for a good long while. Hal had followed Jeff out, leaving Casey and Rose alone in the big room.

"Hal insists the island is secure, but I can't help but feel sort of creeped out after what happened," Casey admitted.

"That's understandable," Rose said in a subdued voice. "I feel the same."

"Would you…" Casey trailed off, then seemed to shake off her reticence and went on. "Would you see it if something else was going to happen tonight?"

Rose had to shake her head. "It doesn't quite work that way. I see some events, but by no means all."

"That's a shame," Casey said quickly, rubbing her arms as if she was cold, yet the room was at a comfortable temperature. It was nerves, Rose knew. She was feeling a bit shaky herself, still.

Jeff poked his head into the room for a moment and told them to sit tight. Rose saw a group of soldiers she'd never met before walking quickly down the main hallway behind him, heading for the mess hall. Most of the men were wearing gear that denoted them as MPs or Military Police, and there was at least one highly ranked officer with them. As they passed behind Jeff, Jeana appeared in the doorway, and he ushered her in then shut the door, leaving the three women alone.

"Jeana!" Casey said, rushing forward to give the doctor a nervous hug. "I thought you were supposed to stay at the base commander's place tonight."

"I would have," Jeana said as Casey stepped back, "but Hal called the commander's house and said something about a prisoner. Commander Kinkaid rushed right over, and he figured I might as well come back here with him. The whole place is on high alert, though they're really good at stealth. You wouldn't know it from outside, but every soldier on this base is on guard tonight. Kinkaid has a way with his people. They'd do just about anything for him." Jeana sounded admiring of the base commander's skill. "Tell me what happened?"

Casey launched into a description of events from which Rose stood back and only spoke when asked for her perspective. She was on edge. Something about the prisoner and the way he had been sniffing around had sent up a red flag in the back of her mind. She was glad she'd told Jeff about it, and she hoped he could get to the bottom of whatever it was. She didn't think she'd get any answers tonight, but she hoped, in time, someone would tell her what the sniffing thing was all about. It felt significant.

After the flow of adrenaline that had kept her hyper aware for the past hours, Rose knew she was crashing hard. She wanted her bed. But, more than that, she wanted to see Jeff. To hold him in her arms and be certain he was whole and unharmed. She wanted him in her bed, holding her, all night long.

She drifted toward the doorway to the big hall while the other two women gravitated toward the sofas on the other side of the room. They were still talking about the events of the night, but Rose felt compelled to look out into the hall. She cracked the door open and immediately realized they were transporting the prisoner. He was bound to a gurney and handcuffed, his wrists and feet attached to the steel frame of the rolling stretcher, even as he thrashed and tried to break free.

He was like a wild man, and his eyes glowed with yellow fire as they met hers. She stood silent, shocked in the doorway, and he stilled.

"This isn't over, Pythia," he growled. She swore she heard a beast in his voice as he leveled her with his gaze. Could the man inspire fear with his voice alone? That would never do.

Not sure of what she was doing, but feeling compelled to do it, nonetheless, Rose stepped fully into the hallway. The men pushing the gurney slowed as time seemed to become sluggish. Jeff was near, and she met his gaze. He seemed to be watching with attentive eyes as she turned her attention back to the prisoner.

"It's over for you," she told him, not certain where her surety or bravado was coming from.

"I'd like to see them try to hold me," he replied, his voice becoming even gruffer.

She held out one hand, not sure why she did so, but feeling she must. Words came to her, and it occurred to her that she was speaking them aloud, even if she didn't fully understand what she was saying.

"I bind you to this form, until you allow the Light to purify your soul."

Every eye in the place turned to her as she spoke, including all of Jeff's co-workers and a few men she didn't know, including the base commander. The moment she was done speaking, the man on the gurney let out an inhuman roar.

"You! You can't do this to me!" he screamed at her, but she felt like something bigger and more powerful than any of them was guiding her actions. "The war isn't over. It'll never be over! The Destroyer will eat you alive. All of you! She will have your powers for her own. You cannot stand in the face of her supremacy."

"Bullshit," Hal swore, moving to Jeff's side and looking down at the prisoner. "We stopped you here, and we will stop you wherever we find you. Your time is over." Hal looked up at the men pushing the gurney and gave the signal for them to go. "Move out. He's going to a cell, and nowhere else."

"He's not much danger now," Commander Kinkaid said to the men, coming around the gurney as it moved forward. He stood in front of Rose, blocking her view of the prisoner, which she considered a favor, since she wasn't sure she could take much more of his wild eyes and crazy talk. "Miss Kitsapolous? I'm Commander Kinkaid." The commander held out his hand for a shake.

She felt a little tingle of power from the man as their hands touched, but he felt clean. Good. Somehow...magical?

She shook her head. It had been a long, stressful day. Her mind was playing tricks on her. Although...

"I've never seen that done before, ma'am, and I was wondering if that's a skill you've always had, or is it something new?" Kinkaid asked.

"You mean...?" She was finding it hard to put into words. "The thing I just said? To be honest, I'm not sure what that was about. It felt like something was speaking through me."

Kinkaid frowned a bit. "Has that happened to you before?"

"Occasionally, but not often. Usually, it's when something vitally important is at stake. Do you know what those words did here?" She was really curious about what she'd felt happen. Something. Something had definitely happened, but she wasn't sure exactly what.

"You froze him in his human form," Kinkaid said simply, keeping his voice pitched lower so that only Hal, Jeff and she could hear.

"I did what now?" She gave the commander a skeptical look.

"Come now, Miss Kitsapolous. You saw his eyes. You heard the voice. That man is a shapeshifter."

Kinkaid didn't look insane. But...he had to be wrong. Didn't he?

"Um..." Rose didn't know what to say to that.

"Jeeves here told the captain about the sniffing activity you've noticed in the past. While it's not common knowledge, you are already part of a world in which you seem to have very little true knowledge. That needs to change if you're going to be a warrior for Light." Kinkaid seemed so earnest. She wanted to believe he was nuts, but his words held a ring of truth, and his manner was very convincing. "I wasn't told much about this unit before you all descended on the island, but I'm beginning to understand why you were placed here. Captain, I'd like to meet with you and these two tomorrow after breakfast. There are some harsh truths that need to be spoken, and decisions made. For now, I'll take charge of the prisoner. I know how to deal with his kind."

"We'll need to question him," Hal put in, somewhat disrespectfully, but the commander let it pass.

"Son, he will be questioned, but not by the likes of us. When supernatural powers are involved, it takes specialist help, which luckily, we have. I'll report back to Admiral Morrow tonight, and tomorrow, we'll have our little powwow. Don't worry. This isn't my first rodeo." The commander sent Rose a smile then walked out the door after the gurney.

Hal gave Rose a puzzled look but didn't say anything. He just shook his head then headed into the room behind her to reunite with Casey. That left Jeff with Rose as the hallway cleared out. The rest of the unit was going about their business, securing things and helping make sure the prisoner was well guarded, but they left Jeff alone with Rose, which was all that mattered to her at the moment.

Jeff simply opened has arms, and Rose stepped into his embrace. Where she'd wanted to be for hours.

"Are you okay?" he asked, rocking her gently from side to side.

"I'm fine, now," she told him. "But I was scared, Jeff. Really scared."

"I know. But you worked through the fear and did what you had to do, regardless. That's bravery, sweet Rosie, and I couldn't admire you more." His words were low, his praise genuine. It touched her heart.

"You're the brave one, fighting that man. I'm so glad you're all right." She pushed back to look at him. "You are okay, right?

Jeff decided Rosie didn't need to hear about his aches and pains, though his wrist still hurt like a son of a bitch. He was pretty sure it wasn't broken, though, because he could still move it, and the pain was lessening. The bruises would color up tomorrow if they weren't already turning black and blue right now, but they were nothing. He would walk through fire—literally—to keep her safe. She was that important to him.

Suddenly, he couldn't hold his feelings in anymore. Too much had happened. Too much might still happen. He wanted to tell her how much he cared for her before anything else interfered.

"I love you, Rosie," he whispered, looking deep into her eyes. They widened as she heard his words.

"You do?"

Jeff swallowed against the dryness in his throat. She'd been brave. Now, it was his turn.

"I do," he assured her. "I truly do."

Her smile lit the universe. "I love you, too." She laughed, and he felt a smile stretch his own lips. "I know it's crazy. We've only just met, but my feelings... They're strong, and they're real. I've never felt this way before."

"Me neither," he told her, grinning like a fool as she caught him after his leap of faith.

A noise in the distance made him check their surroundings. They were alone for the moment, but that would change if they stayed in the middle of the main hallway.

"The rest of the guys can handle things from here," he said quickly, knowing they would cover for him. "Let's go someplace else." He meant someplace private, and from the twinkle in her eyes, she fully understood his intent.

Jeff took her hand and they nearly jogged down the hallways that led to her quarters.

CHAPTER ELEVEN

The first time they made love was hard and fast. So fast it nearly took the top of Rose's head off as her climax hit almost without warning. Jeff rolled them on the bed so that she draped over him like a living blanket as their breathing went from rapid to more reasonable.

His hand stroking her back felt so good. He was so warm and delicious beneath her. Rose felt her interest perking up again. That first climax had just taken the edge off, but she was still hungry for more, she found, once she'd had a chance to catch her breath.

She rubbed against him, discovering the hardness against her inner thigh that meant he was feeling the same. Rose smiled, licking his throat, enjoying the saltiness of his skin as he groaned.

"Ready for more?" His voice rumbled through his chest and against her body, even as his rough tone caressed her ears.

"You know it," she replied, squirming around, searching for what she wanted.

He reached downward and made things easier, positioning himself for her. She slid downward and took him inside. Yes. That's what she wanted. That's what she needed. Him. Only him. Forever.

Shocked a little by her own thoughts, Rose stilled for a moment, but then, Jeff touched her clit, and she was off and running. Riding him like a jockey, heading for the finish line. She rose up on her elbows, then her hands, using any leverage she could to make the contact between their bodies even more intense.

It didn't take long. Not when she was able to control the motion. She cried out and shuddered on top of him, coming hard. Then, it was his turn.

Jeff rolled them over again, but instead of taking the position they had before, with him on top and her on her back, he changed things up. He flipped her then lifted her to her knees, putting her ass up in the air as he moved behind. Doggy style had its advantages. Rose gathered a pillow to her and leaned up on her elbows as he began ramming into her from behind.

She cried out again, making another climax that was even higher than the one just past. She hadn't known her body was capable of such pleasure...until Jeff. Each time she was with him, she learned something new about herself. About him. About the limits and reaches of pleasure.

This time was no different. She came again—this time, with him as he stiffened and probed deep within her, coming hard. When he was finally spent, he repositioned them like spoons, cuddling her as one hand absently stroked her hip.

"I don't ever want this to end," he whispered near her ear.

"Me neither," she agreed, feeling tingly at the hint of forever in his words.

He was silent a moment, then he moved, levering himself upward in the bed. She rolled over onto her back so she could look up at him, meeting his gaze. His beautiful blue eyes were so serious.

"Do you mean it?" he asked. She didn't need clarification. She suddenly knew he was, indeed, talking about something more permanent between them.

"I do," she said, unconsciously echoing the words she really wanted to say in a much more formal setting. He seemed to understand. Jeff smiled, his eyes nearly glowing with happiness.

"I'll want to hear you say that again, in front of a priest. And wearing something besides your beautiful smile," he teased.

"I will, if you'd just ask me, already!" she replied, sitting up in the bed as he slid off the side. She moved to sit on the side of the bed as he knelt before her.

"Sweet, sweet, Rosie, will you marry me?

She flung herself into his arms, and they ended up on the floor. Thank goodness, it had been newly carpeted as part of Casey's redecorating scheme.

"Yes!" she whispered into his ear as she hugged him tight. "Yes, yes, yes!"

"I love you so much, Rosie. You've brought meaning to my life and helped make sense of the changes. I want you with me, forever, the way I see you in my dreams," he admitted, making her heart leap.

"Dreams?" she asked, moving back slightly to look into his eyes. "Or visions?"

"Both," he confirmed, taking her breath away. "My daydreams of the future and my visions of what will come," he added before joining his lips to hers in the sweetest kiss she had ever known.

He'd seen them together in his visions. He'd come for her because he'd foreseen their love, their passion, their future. Rose had never been happier in her life, and she suspected that sensation would return to her many times as the years passed, with Jeff by her side.

She was a lucky, blessed, fortunate girl.

*

The next morning, Hal accompanied Jeff and Rose to the base commander's office. Commander Lester Kinkaid was ready for them and got right down to business.

"As I said last night, I wasn't sure why your

unit was assigned here at first, but I've since had a long discussion with Admiral Morrow, and he's cleared up a few things. First, I must remind you that you are all under obligation not to reveal or discuss anything you may learn while on this base—ever. If that was not already made clear to your men, Captain Haliwell, I expect you'll be certain the message is received. That also includes you, Miss Kitsapolous. The employment contract you signed yesterday with Dr. Holbrook contains that language, in case you don't remember, or didn't read it closely enough."

Rose nodded. "I read it, and I understand."

"Good. Now, you need to know that I've been briefed on what happened to your unit in the ancient city of Babylon," Kinkaid began.

Rose saw Hal's reaction to that news, though he tried to hide it. He was concerned. Apparently, the things that had happened to him and his men were not things he wanted just anyone to know.

"I know this isn't common knowledge, nor should it be, but Admiral Morrow felt I needed to know so we could work together. He also cleared me to make you aware of the special nature of this installation and the people who live and work here." It was Kinkaid's turn to frown. "That's not something I do lightly, so you may consider us even, once you hear what I have to say."

Hal kept silent, as did Jeff and Rose. Whatever the commander was about to tell them, it was his story to tell, and he was still in charge. Rose might not be military, but she understood chain of command. She didn't want to get on Kinkaid's bad side. From what she'd seen last night and this morning, he was a very capable man who didn't suffer fools gladly. Or, maybe, she was just imagining that last bit because of his gruff manner. She hadn't seen him mad at anyone, so she supposed she ought to keep a more open mind.

"The thing is, every person on this base has some extrasensory ability." Kinkaid dropped that verbal bomb and let silence reign for a moment.

So much for that open mind thing, Rose thought carefully to herself. This guy just had to be nuts. Then again… It would explain a lot.

"So, there are more like us, sir?" Hal asked, better able to control his surprise than Rose would be in his shoes.

Kinkaid shook his head. "Not exactly like your unit, Captain. There are other…shall we say, supernatural…abilities in play. Some of the personnel assigned here are shapeshifters of one kind or another. Some have mixed ancestry that allows them to access what you might call magic. I oversee their development and utilization, but the operatives on this base are either highly specialized solo operatives or background personnel that support the others in the field. Knowing this, you'll probably soon realize, if it hasn't occurred to you already, that there are entire Special Forces units made up of shapeshifters. You've probably crossed paths with some of them on past ops."

Rose felt a shiver down her spine, and a sudden knowing overtook her. It happened sometimes. She felt compelled to speak of what she saw, regardless of military protocol. She thought maybe her gift would help cut through some of the questions and disbelief she was feeling, so she went with her instincts.

"I see you, Commander," she said, drawing the attention of the men. "You and a...big sea lion?"

"Seal," Kinkaid corrected her, coughing slightly. "I'm a selkie."

"Like in the Irish legends?" she asked, her eyes still unfocused as she received impressions. "But that's not all. There's a lion, too. A massive lion with a dark mane."

Kinkaid whistled between his teeth. "I can see it would be hard to keep secrets from you, ma'am. I'm a rarity in the shifter world. I have two animal spirits. I can be either the lion or the seal. It's not common, and it's why Morrow put me in charge here. I have unique perspective on land and sea." Kinkaid looked from Rose to Jeff, as if wanting some reaction.

Jeff finally shook his head, just slightly. "Apologies, sir, but this is hard to believe," he finally said in a low, troubled voice.

Commander Kinkaid stood and went over to the door of his office. "I know. Which is why I've asked one of my Clan mates to give you a demonstration." The commander opened the door, and a five-hundred-pound lion strolled into the room, calm as you please.

Jeff and Hal both jumped to their feet. Jeff

stood in a ready position, directly in front of Rose, protecting her. It was sweet, but she had to lean around him in her seat to see the magnificent beast that seemed amused by Jeff's actions, if Rose was any judge. Kinkaid was just shaking his head.

"Stand down," Kinkaid advised, but neither Hal nor Jeff relaxed their stance. "This is Liam. My son. Show 'em, son."

What little Rose could see of the lion around Jeff's back started to shimmer, and an intense tingling sensation seemed to flow through her body from the cat's direction. A shimmering cloud of smoke appeared, and then, a moment later, it resolved into the shape of a man. A very big man. A very naked man.

The commander tossed the newcomer a beach towel that had been lying on a side table. It was dark blue terrycloth with a Navy logo on it, and big enough to wrap around the man's trim waist a couple of times. He covered up and leaned against the doorjamb, one hip cocked at a jaunty angle. Hal seemed to relax a bit, but Jeff's stance didn't change. He was still wound tight, taking in this new—astounding—information.

Rose pushed her chair back and stood, putting her hand on Jeff's tense shoulder as she moved to stand next to him. She felt her way in this new situation, letting her instincts guide her. She sensed no hostility from this Liam, nor had she sensed anything dangerous from the big cat he had, incredibly, just been. She looked at the bare-chested man and smiled as best she could.

"That was quite an entrance. I'm Rose," she introduced herself.

The man smiled, his tawny eyes focusing on her, his expression amused. "Liam Kinkaid," he said, reaching out his hand. She took it for a friendly shake and was immediately hit with a vision.

"Danger surrounds you," she said, as the man let go of her hand. The image didn't weaken in her mind's eye. It grew stronger. "A woman in black. An enemy steeped in evil. Beware. They are hunting you both."

"When?"

The question came from the commander, not his son. Rose took a look around the vision before it faded, for clues as to timing.

"When the moon is full and there is a sprinkling of snow on the ground. In a pine forest. Massive pines. Like Giant Sequoia, or something. I've never seen anything like them. One especially magical tree that is taller than any tree I've ever seen. It dominates the forest. It will shelter you, if you let it. Evil cannot penetrate its ancient aura. Snow dusts its branches as it falls, but there's not much on the ground. A first snowfall? Full moon high in the sky. A huge owl in a nearby tree, watching. No other landmarks, sorry." Even as she spoke, the vision faded. "That's all."

"You're a seer," Liam said, his expression bemused.

Well, that answered one of the questions in her mind. Apparently, not everyone on the island had been told about her abilities.

"What about you, Lieutenant?" the commander asked Jeff.

"Sorry, sir. I didn't get any of that. Rose's skills are a bit broader-spectrum than mine, it seems. And more finely honed."

The commander nodded. "Which is why she was put on the payroll. Makes sense. You'll learn we have a number of consultants here on the island teaching our operatives various specialized skills. Now that we're all on the same page, we can share resources a bit. From what the admiral tells me, there should be some areas of overlap between our two commands," he said to Hal. Then, he gave his son an offhand command. "Liam, go put on your uniform again, and come back. I want you to be my liaison with Captain Haliwell's unit."

Liam left the room as everybody sat back down again. "Bit unorthodox, isn't it?" Hal said quietly to the commander. "Having family members under your command, I mean."

Kinkaid shook his head. "It's the only way for some of us. Depending on species, we shifters adhere to a hierarchy. Around here, I'm the Alpha. My son knows this, and his inner beast respects it as truth. Without an Alpha to follow and respect, many shifters couldn't participate in the military. Admiral Morrow knows this, and it's why he personally handles all the Spec Ops units and teams that have specialized talents. Which is why he's now your go-to, as well, Captain."

"I'd always heard good things about the

admiral, even if I never served under him before," Hal answered diplomatically.

They were dancing around what Rose really wanted to know, but she wasn't constrained by military protocol. She cleared her throat delicately, which had the effect of drawing attention her way.

"Is the admiral a...um...shifter, too?" she asked, using her most polite tone. She didn't want to piss off a man who could turn into a lion, and—military protocol aside—she wasn't sure what was appropriate when conversing with a shapeshifter. She supposed she'd have to learn.

"Generally speaking, such questions aren't asked among magical folk. We prefer subtlety and mystery. Of course, I'm a cat, so maybe my kind takes it to extremes," Kinkaid answered with a friendly smile. "But you're new to all this, and I understand that. We'll make allowances until you all get up to speed." He addressed his words to all of them now. "As for the admiral, he's not a shifter, but few know exactly what he is. He's even more mysterious than most cats I know." Kinkaid's smile softened his words.

"I apologize if I was rude. As you said, I have a lot to learn," Rose offered.

The commander shook his head and made a brushing gesture with one hand that told her he hadn't taken offense.

"We all do," Jeff said, covering her hand with his. "And sirs, there is something Rose and I want to make clear." He took a deep breath and plunged ahead. "We're engaged."

Hal started chuckling as the commander smiled. "Son, to a shifter, your bond was obvious the moment you walked within sniffing distance, but I'm happy to hear you've made it official in the eyes of man. Since my command is a bit non-traditional, I don't have any problem with the two of you continuing to work together." Commander Kinkaid looked expectantly at Hal. "Captain? What do you say?"

"I'm hardly in a position to complain. Not with Casey living on base with me," Hal replied. "Congratulations, you two." He offered Jeff his hand for a friendly shake then lifted Rose's hand for a quick kiss as he smiled and winked at her over the back of her hand. She could feel his true happiness for Jeff and her. It was heartwarming.

A view of the future settled into her mind for a brief moment. It was a happy picture of Jeff and his friends—most of whom had a woman by their side. Casey was there, as was Dr. Holbrook, and the woman from the mall who had been behind the kiosk. Others Rose didn't recognize but knew she would know in time. Everybody looked happy, sharing a meal together in the mess hall.

That was it, then. For the foreseeable future, Rose and Jeff would forge their path together, on this island, with his unit of friends who had grown into family.

"Did you see that?" Jeff asked her in a whisper as the younger Kinkaid opened the door and drew everyone else's attention.

"Dinner with your friends?" she asked in just as low a tone as she smiled at him.

His eyes were wide, his expression astonished. "Who were all those women?"

"Girlfriends, fiancées, and wives, I believe," she replied, a teasing smile on her face.

"What did I miss?" Liam asked, as he settled into a chair to the side of his father's desk.

The commander looked at Jeff and Rose with a raised eyebrow. "You two just saw something, didn't you?"

Jeff squeezed Rose's hand, and she decided to field the question. "Sometimes, Commander, we will keep our visions to ourselves until the time is right, because sometimes, it isn't good for others to know what will happen. They might do something to alter the future into an unforeseen path. In this case, though, I think it's safe to say that we both just had a glimpse of the future for Captain Haliwell's unit, and it was a very bright future, indeed."

EPILOGUE

Jeff was doing PT with the rest of the unit one morning a few days later and ended up standing next to Carter, who had just rejoined the unit after the gunshot wound in his leg had been healed by the unit's doctor, Rick. Carter had been shot in the mall when they'd liberated Rose, and Jeff had thanked him for the sacrifice.

Carter had also been the man left behind with Hannah, the cast-footed kiosk attendant. Apparently, the local emergency services had insisted on treating Carter's wound, and he'd only managed to sign himself out of their hospital the day before. He'd come right back to the island where Rick had used his freaky new healing skills to fix up his arm like new.

"Heard anything about Hannah?" Jeff asked

Carter as nonchalantly as possible. He knew from his own new gift that Hannah might play a very important role in Carter's life in the future, if he'd let her.

"I talked to her before I left the hospital. She visited me to see how I was doing." Carter's tone was filled with surprise that the woman would do that for him.

"How's her foot coming along?" Jeff knew just the right questions to ask, thanks to his vision of the day before, which Rose had helped him interpret.

Carter frowned. "She's been going to the VA for it, but something's wrong with the way it's healing. Did you know she was a vet? She served in Afghanistan and was wounded by a roadside bomb. That's how her foot got messed up in the first place. Her tour was almost up, and after that, she decided to try civilian life again."

"Can't blame her. Especially if the foot isn't healing," Jeff said, dropping to the sandy beach to do pushups, as did Carter and the rest of the unit. "Maybe Rick could take a look," Jeff added, as if just thinking of it. In reality, he'd planned what to say to Carter, with Rose's input, last night. They both suspected the guy would need a little nudge in the right direction, and Jeff had just delivered it.

"I wonder if the Cap'n would allow it?" Carter mused aloud.

"Only one way to find out. You should ask him. She did see us in action, so it's not like she doesn't know who we are. And she's a vet.

Rick's talent is going to waste out here with just us to look after. I bet he'd be happy to help her," Jeff added.

"You're right." Carter got a determined look in his eye, which made Jeff want to smile, but he wisely held it in. "I'll look into it after breakfast."

"Good man."

Jeff secretly aimed a thumbs-up to where he knew Rosie—his beloved fiancée—was watching from the mess hall windows. Seeing the future was one thing, but learning how to use the information to help others... That was the real skill. Rosie did it by instinct and with her open and kind heart. She was teaching him that, and so much else about love and trust and being with someone who was perfect for him in every possible way.

When he'd first seen Rosie, he'd guessed there was something special about her. Now, after loving her, he had no doubt.

ABOUT THE AUTHOR

Bianca D'Arc has run a laboratory, climbed the corporate ladder in the shark-infested streets of lower Manhattan, studied and taught martial arts, and earned the right to put a whole bunch of letters after her name, but she's always enjoyed writing more than any of her other pursuits. She grew up and still lives on Long Island, where she keeps busy with an extensive garden, several aquariums full of very demanding fish, and writing her favorite genres of paranormal, fantasy and sci-fi romance.

Bianca loves to hear from readers and can be reached through Twitter (@BiancaDArc), Facebook (BiancaDArcAuthor) or through the various links on her website.

WELCOME TO THE D'ARC SIDE…
WWW.BIANCADARC.COM

OTHER BOOKS BY BIANCA D'ARC

PARANORMAL ROMANCE

Brotherhood of Blood
One & Only
Rare Vintage
Phantom Desires
Sweeter Than Wine
Forever Valentine
Wolf Hills*
Wolf Quest

Tales of the Were
Lords of the Were
Inferno
Rocky
Slade

Tales ~ Redstone Clan
The Purrfect Stranger
Grif
Red
Magnus
Bobcat
Matt

Tales ~ String of Fate
Cat's Cradle
King's Throne
Jacob's Ladder
Her Warriors

Tales ~ Grizzly Cove
All About the Bear
Mating Dance
Night Shift
Alpha Bear
Saving Grace
Bearliest Catch
The Bear's Healing Touch
The Luck of the Shifters
Badass Bear
Bounty Hunter Bear
Storm Bear
Bear Meets Girl
Spirit Bear
Lion in Waiting

Tales ~ Gemini Project
Tag Team
Doubling Down
Deuces Wild

Tales ~
Gifts of the Ancients
Warrior's Heart
Future Past

Tales ~
Were-Fey Trilogy
Lone Wolf
Snow Magic
Midnight Kiss

Tales ~
Lick of Fire Trilogy
Phoenix Rising
Phoenix and the Wolf
Phoenix and the
Dragon

Tales ~
Howls Romance
The Jaguar Tycoon
The Jaguar
Bodyguard
The Jaguar's Secret
Baby

Tales ~ Big Wolf
A Touch of Class

**Guardians of the
Dark**
Simon Says
Once Bitten
Smoke on the Water
Night Shade
Shadow Play

**EPIC FANTASY
EROTIC ROMANCE**

Dragon Knights ~
**Daughters of the
Dragon**
Maiden Flight*
Border Lair
The Ice Dragon**
Prince of Spies***

Dragon Knights ~
The Novellas
The Dragon Healer
Master at Arms
Wings of Change

Dragon Knights ~
Sons of Draconia
FireDrake
Dragon Storm
Keeper of the Flame
Hidden Dragons

The Sea Captain's
Daughter Trilogy
Sea Dragon
Dragon Fire
Dragon Mates

The Captain's Dragon

SCIENCE FICTION ROMANCE

StarLords
Hidden Talent
Talent For Trouble
Shy Talent

Jit'Suku Chronicles
~
In the Stars
The Cyborg Next Door
Heart of the Machine

Jit'Suku Chronicles
~ Arcana
King of Swords
King of Cups
King of Clubs
King of Stars
End of the Line
Diva

Jit'Suku Chronicles ~
Sons of Amber
Angel in the Badlands
Master of Her Heart

FUTURISTIC EROTIC ROMANCE

Resonance Mates
Hara's Legacy**
Davin's Quest
Jaci's Experiment
Grady's Awakening
Harry's Sacrifice

CONTEMPORARY ROMANCE

Irish Lullaby
Bells Will Be Ringing
Wild Irish Rose

* RT Book Reviews
Awards Nominee
** EPPIE Award Winner
*** CAPA Award Winner

LONE WOLF

Josh is a werewolf who suddenly has extra, unexpected and totally untrained powers. He's not happy about it - or about the evil jackasses who keep attacking him, trying to steal his magic. Forced to seek help, Josh is sent to an unexpected ally for training.

Deena is a priestess with more than her share of magical power and a unique ability that has made her a target. She welcomes Josh, seeing a kindred soul in the lone werewolf. She knows she can help him... if they can survive their enemies long enough.

SNOW MAGIC

Evie has been a lone wolf since the disappearance of her mate, Sir Rayburne, a fey knight from another realm. Left all alone with a young son to raise, Evie has become stronger than she ever was. But now her son is grown and suddenly Ray is back.

Ray never meant to leave Evie all those years ago but he's been caught in a magical trap, slowly being drained of magic all this time. Freed at last, he whisks Evie to the only place he knows in the mortal realm where they were happy and safe—the rustic cabin in the midst of a North Dakota winter where they had been newlyweds. He's used the last of his magic to get there and until he recovers a bit, they're stuck in the middle of nowhere with a blizzard coming and bad guys on their trail.

Can they pick up where they left off and rekindle the magic between them, or has it been extinguished forever?

MIDNIGHT KISS

Margo is a werewolf on a mission...with a disruptively handsome mage named Gabe. She can't figure out where Gabe fits in the pecking order, but it doesn't seem to matter to the attraction driving her wild. Gabe knows he's going to have to prove himself in order to win Margo's heart. He wants her for his mate, but can she give her heart to a mage? And will their dangerous quest get in the way?

PHOENIX RISING

Lance is inexplicably drawn to the sun and doesn't understand why. Tina is a witch who remembers him from their high school days. She'd had a crush on the quiet boy who had an air of magic about him. Reunited by Fate, she wonders if she could be the one to ground him and make him want to stay even after the fire within him claims his soul...if only their love can be strong enough.

PHOENIX AND THE WOLF

Diana is drawn to the sun and dreams of flying, but her elderly grandmother needs her feet firmly on the ground. When Diana's old clunker breaks down in front of a high-end car lot, she seeks help and finds herself ensnared by the sexy werewolf mechanic who runs the repair shop. Stone makes her want to forget all her responsibilities and take a walk on the wild side...with him.

PHOENIX AND THE DRAGON

He's a dragon shapeshifter in search of others like himself. She's a newly transformed phoenix shifter with a lot to learn and bad guys on her trail. Together, they will go on a dazzling adventure into the unknown, and fight against evil folk intent on subduing her immense power and using it for their own ends. They will face untold danger and find love that will last a lifetime.

THE JAGUAR TYCOON

Mark may be the larger-than-life billionaire Alpha of the secretive Jaguar Clan, but he's a pussycat when it comes to the one women destined to be his mate. Shelly is an up-and-coming architect trying to drum up business at an elite dinner party at which Mark is the guest of honor. When shots ring out, the hunt for the gunman brings Mark into Shelly's path and their lives will never be the same.

THE JAGUAR BODYGUARD

Sworn to protect his Clan, Nick heads to Hollywood to keep an eye on a rising star who has seen a little too much for her own good. Unexpectedly fame has made a circus of Sal's life, but when decapitated squirrels show up on her doorstep, she knows she needs professional help. Nick embeds himself in her security squad to keep an eye on her as sparks fly and passions rise between them. Can he keep her safe and prevent her from revealing what she knows?

THE JAGUAR'S SECRET BABY

Hank has never forgotten the wild woman with whom he spent one memorable night. He's dreamed of her for years now, but has never been back to the small airport in Texas owned and run by her werewolf Pack. Tracy was left with a delicious memory of her night in Hank's arms, and a beautiful baby girl who is the light of her life. She chose not to tell Hank about his daughter, but when he finally returns and he discovers the daughter he's never known, he'll do all he can to set things right.

DRAGON KNIGHTS

Two dragons, two knights, and one woman to complete their circle. That's the recipe for happiness in the land of fighting dragons. But there are a few special dragons that are more. They are the ruling family and they are half-dragon and half-human, able to change at will from one form to another.

Books in this series have won the EPPIE Award for Best Erotic Romance in the Fantasy/Paranormal category, and have been nominated for RT Book Reviews Magazine Reviewers Choice Awards among other honors.

WWW.BIANCADARC.COM